MY LADY

First published 2021

A self published title
Designed and produced by Adala Publishing
www.adala.com.au

Cover artwork by Claire Chancellor

A catalogue record for this book is available from the National Library of Australia

ISBN 978-0-6487116-6-7 (Print)
ISBN 978-0-6487116-7-4 (eBook)

MY LADY

TREVOR L EVANS

ADALA
PUBLISHING

I dedicate this book to all of those who are now entering retirement, you have planned your retirement well, but you are now about to enter no-mans land. The horizon belongs to you.

It is no longer somebody else's horizon, it is yours, you are stronger, the knowledge you have gained through life is yours, not for others to use, your mind is your own.

The book is about John and Mary and their journey into retirement, and the forces working for them to make their retirement so successful.

Take your shoes off and step aboard, sit down on the cushions where you are comfortable and feel the warmth of the sun and read this book…

I STOOD IN front of the big glass window, 30 storeys in the air, looking down at Sydney harbour. I could see the ferries and many small sailing vessels. I could see the Sydney Harbour Bridge, the Opera House, cars, and people looking like ants. Sydney is alive; it is a beautiful city. Nowhere in the world is there another city quite like Sydney. Nowhere else would you find a beautiful harbour like this that attracts people from all over the world.

There was a knock at the door. 'Come in.' The door opened and Terry, a colleague of mine, walked in.

'Good Morning, John. How are you?'

'Come in Terry. Sit down. How am I? Full of mixed feelings!'

'John, while I have the chance to be alone with you, I've just come to say thank you. You have always supported me, always stood by me at the board meetings. You haven't always agreed with me, but you've always given me a sound logical reason as to why. You've always looked at the problem from both sides, and when I have made my decisions you have supported me, so thank you for the years, John.'

'Terry, I've always found you to be a very fair man, a man of high principles and integrity, and I love the way you play the politics.'

'Well John, if there is anything I can do for you in the future, in your retirement, please let me know.'

'Thank you, Terry, thank you.'

Terry stood up from the chair and as we shook hands, he slapped me on the shoulder with his other hand. 'John, I will miss watching you play chess with the rest of the board members!' After he left, I sat down in my worn-out swivel chair. It was so comfortable; made of timber with green leather padding. The big boss Walter had given it to me many years ago, but he had now passed away. He built the company from nothing, starting with a wheelbarrow delivering flour to bakeries. He had a charm with people like no other man I have ever known. I first met him when I was 16 years old, cleaning out the hulls of ships, ready for their next cargo.

It wasn't long before I became a foreman, then supervisor. I eventually went into management, climbing the greasy ladder to the top, and now I was the big boss man. I only answered to the directors, who gave me free rein. They were too busy playing golf, going to lunches, and playing politics with politicians. I had decided a long time ago that there was a retirement age. Now my time had come; I must step aside. I looked around the room fighting back tears. I looked at the photo of Walter on the wall. In my mind's eye I thought he was grinning at me. All the furniture and the desk in this room had been his.

There was a knock at the door. Margaret, my secretary walked in with a cup of coffee in her hand.

'Your coffee Sir.'

'Margaret, don't ever call me sir again. To you, my name is John. We've been together for so long, you have been my constant companion, I will always be grateful to you.'

She clasped her hands together and looked at her feet.

'No, no, Margaret. If you break down, and I, well, I have too much to do, and I must be in control of myself.' I opened a drawer in my desk and took out a large envelope. 'Margaret, this is a retirement package I have put together for you. You will retire in one month. That gives you time to work with my… well, you know what I mean. Margaret, will you help him to take command. These papers have been signed by all the directors so that nobody can change your package. Now, Margaret, do you have those boxes for me?'

She gave me a cheeky smile, and a sweet and dainty curtsy. 'Yes Sir, John.' She disappeared through the door and returned with some boxes. She set them down alongside me, gave me another little curtsy and a warm smile.

I'd never seen her like this before. She had always been straight and businesslike. I knew now we were friends. I started to pack my things into the boxes; papers I wanted to keep, notebooks, silly little things that didn't mean anything to anybody else, but were so precious to me. I picked up an old fountain pen, it was gold and silver; my name was engraved on it and a single word 'Thank you'. Walter had given this to me a long time ago, for keeping secrets.

There was another knock on the door. Ross walked in, he was an arrogant man; sly, and utterly untrustworthy. He was always using other people so that he was not held responsible nor did he get the blame.

'Oh, oh, John, those papers for Manningham Construction, could I have them now?'

I thought to myself, no, you bloody can't! I want someone else to read them first! 'I'm a bit rushed at the moment, and I have things to put together for the board before I leave. I'll get them to you later.'

'John, I'd rather I had them now.' I knew I didn't have to play politics anymore; it was finished.

'I said, I will get the papers to you later. Now, please leave. I am a bit overwhelmed at the moment.' He walked out and slammed the door. I put some more papers in the boxes and taped them up.

The phone rang; it was Margaret. 'I have Frank here for you.'

'Please send him straight in Margaret.'

I stood up to shake Frank's hand. 'Please sit down, Frank.' Frank was the man who was going to take my place; I had trained him; he was the best I could find. One or two of the board members wanted their own man, but I think I played the politics well. I would have loved to be a fly on the wall to see Frank play his chess game with them. No doubt, it will get back to me. 'Frank, you take over first thing in the morning, don't you?'

'Yes John, I do. John, that dear friend of ours who just left your office slamming the door behind him seemed to be in such a big hurry that he tripped over one of your boxes and his toupee slid down over the front of his face. Your two ladies held their composure extremely well. I never knew he wore a toupee, and I don't think anyone else did either. It isn't a secret anymore.'

With a grin I handed Frank the Manningham contract. 'Frank, I would suggest you read over this very carefully. Our friend, who has just left the office, wants it back and I don't think it's in our interests, or should I say, the Company's interest. We've discussed everything you need to know; I'm going to leave this chair for you if you'd like it.'

'Yes, John, I would certainly like to have your chair when you retire. I would appreciate it.'

'Now Frank I will show you something interesting about this desk. If you pull the top draw out, put your hand inside underneath the desktop you will find a little lever. Pull that lever like this.'

A little drawer, which was hidden in the fancy woodwork, slid out. 'This desk was Walters; he showed it to me. You and I are the only ones who know the draw is here. I have put some CDs together with information on every person within the company structure. These CDs will help you survive. I'm quite sure there will be some individuals in the enterprise who think this information may be in the vault. So I will leave that to you.'

'Thank you, John; I will go through them carefully.' Frank held out his hand and I shook it.

'Good luck Frank. I know you will play the game well.'

'I'll see you at the party John.'

'Yes, and we will have a drink together.'

As Frank closed my office door on his way out I heard the latch click. Sadness came over me; this is the end. I was once the big man at the top of the ladder. Everybody did exactly as I told them. I could spend big money, make big decisions that affected so many others; their incomes, their lives. If they wanted to get to the top, they needed to play the game, my way, my rules. The company house, car, expense account, use of the private jet. It's all gone now. What does the future have for Mary and me?

The rest of the day went by very quickly. We had lunch in the boardroom with only polite chit-chat as I was of no use to them anymore; Frank was now the man. Now and again Frank's eyes caught mine and I knew he was into the politics. He was now in the deep end; they were trying to win his side, his favour. I knew I'd chosen the right man.

After lunch, I was back in my office marking the boxes. I stood at the big windows that overlooked Sydney; a sense of pride came over me. I looked at the Opera House; I had a big part to play in the construction of it, part of it belongs to me personally, inside of me. I would never stand like this again, in front of these windows, looking at my achievements.

There was a knock at the door; I slowly turned around. My wife Mary was at the door. She is My Lady. She walked over and stood beside me; she held my hand. She knew what was happening to me on the inside. I didn't have to say a word. We both stood looking out across Sydney.

I met Mary when she was 17 and I was 18. We got married when I was just 20. At that time we had nothing. She had always been My Lady. She always dressed appropriately, arranged business dinner parties, talked to the other wives, looked after my business colleagues. She always had everything prepared for me. I cherished her deeply, with a love that I can't explain. I knew she was happy about my retirement; I would be hers again. She wouldn't have to share me with the company and answer to them. We would be free.

'Well, John, time to go home.'

'Yes, dear, it's all finished now.' We turned and walked towards the door. She picked up my jacket and put it on her arm. I walked out the door and did not look back into the office.

'We'll see you at the party, Margaret?'

'Yes, Sir, John.'

'Margaret, I owe you a big bunch of red roses.' Then I did something I had never done to anyone in the office before. I walked over and put my arms around her and held her tight. 'Thank you, Margaret, thank you.'

'Thank you John for my retirement package. I didn't expect that.'

I stood back and watched Margaret wipe the tears from her eyes. Mary put her arms around her.

'Thank you for the long conversations on the telephone, Margaret. Thank you for keeping the secrets.' They both chuckled; that women's chuckle.

I heard myself say, 'What secrets, what secrets?'

'Never mind, dear, secret women's business,' Mary said.

I've heard that term used before, dear, when our daughter was young. It would stand up in court, wouldn't it?'

Soon we were in the building's basement where all the company cars were parked. I had a BMW; it was an old BMW classic, it was one of the first company cars that I had. I loved that car, with its timber, leather seats, and trims. I had fought to keep it. I opened the door and slid into the seat. Mary slid into her seat. The maintenance logbook was on the seat along with an envelope, but all I could think about was having to give this car back, it was a company car, not mine.

Mary opened the envelope and read the note. With a grin she handed me the letter. It was from Frank.

John, the Board and I know how much you love this car. It was officially taken off the books a long time ago and it has been registered under your name. The insurance has been paid and she has been fully serviced. Enjoy her now in your retirement.

On behalf of the board and myself, thank you, John.

PS, how are you going to put up with him, Mary? It was hard enough for us.

Your friend Frank.

We stopped at the exit of the car park. A security guard stepped up to the driver's side window.

'Thank you John for looking after my retirement package, and for looking after me throughout the years.'

'Thank you Michael. I remember when we studied together in the good old days. I think a shovel and broom would most probably break my back now.'

'Yes John, they were the good old days. Enjoy your retirement, you've earned it.'

'Well, keep in touch, Michael. Please stay in touch.'

'Good on you John, good on you.' He walked to the car behind us.

We slowly drove to the home that had been ours for 30 years, but it was no longer our home. In one month we had to hand it back to the company. We had brought up our two children here, Deanna and Robert; both grown up and married now, living their own lives. Robert had said we could live in his house while he and his wife were in Singapore working on a project for the bank. I found that a bit annoying. Mary and I had bought that house, we owned it, but as you probably know, as a parent, you have to think a little differently.

I parked the car. I felt a little lost as I walked into the house. I was still thinking of company problems, and how to solve them. I was having trouble letting go. I shouted to myself, 'It's finished, it's over. The problems are no longer yours. You don't belong there anymore. But it has been my whole life!'

I was standing in front of the mirror in our bedroom, looking at my image… I am what I am, 'you, in the mirror, who are you now? How do I face you in the mirror? Everything has to have a logical answer; what is the solution for me? Where do I go now?'

I had talked about retirement with Mary. We talked about ideas on what we might do, but now, I had come face-to-face with myself in the mirror, and I was frightened; I was scared of the future. The face looked back at me. I stood staring at myself with no answers. A voice behind snapped me back to the moment.

'Come on, dear, have your shower. Do you have your speech ready?'

'No, I don't. I'll say what comes into my mind. Politics don't matter anymore.'

Mary had laid my clothes out on the bed as she usually did. I stood staring at the suit and tie. No, I'm not going to wear a suit or a bloody tie! I picked out another shirt, a pair of trousers and a jacket and shoes, and put them on. Mary walked into the bedroom and stared at me for a moment.

'All right John, you're trying to make a statement, but not that jacket. What about the leather jacket we bought for you last month, that would be appropriate.' I looked at her for a few moments. I wanted to shout. I wanted to let my frustrations go, but this was my Mary.

'Yes, dear.' She got the leather jacket out; I handed her back the one I was wearing and put on the leather one. 'But no tie!'

'All right, John, I will meet you halfway.'

We arrived at the yacht club. I admired the view as we walked up the stairs to the entrance. Once inside I was ushered onto a small stage, and everyone stood up and clapped. Frank stood alongside me.

'Ladies and gentlemen, our John, as you all know, has been at the helm of this company for a very long time. He has done a remarkable job of taking our company into the future. I know

Walter would be very proud of his achievements, but his time to retire has come. John, on behalf of everyone here, thank you, you will be truly missed. Feel free to call in at any time, and if there's any way we can assist you in the future, please don't hesitate to ask.' He stood back and left me there to respond.

'Ladies and gentlemen, friends and companions, many of you have travelled the road alongside me throughout the years, and have stood by me. As a team you could handle any problems that destiny put in our way. When, as an individual, you think that you are number one, you are not, because without a team you are nobody. I know that. I have been one of the team, and I thank all of you for playing the game with me.'

I know I said more, I know that I thanked Mary, but then I was on the floor shaking hands, talking to so many people. My whisky glass was always full, it never seemed to be empty. It was top shelf and I was enjoying it. I wasn't playing politics anymore; I was just talking.

I saw Michael and his wife Genevieve standing over to one side, looking a little out of place. I walked over to them. 'Genevieve, how are you?' I gave her a gentle hug. 'It's been a long time hasn't it since we grew up together. Where did the years go? I never understood why you chose Michael instead of me, just because in those days he was charming, witty, and incredibly handsome.'

She put her arm around Michael and cuddled him tightly, looked him straight in the face and gave a small laugh. 'Yes John, I don't know what happened to him!' He gave her a cheeky grin. Genevieve replied 'Thank you so very much too.'

Somebody was topping up my glass again. I said thank you and took another sip. 'When all of this dies down could we have dinner somewhere, just the four of us; like the good old days.' Michael reached out and put his hand on my shoulder.

'Why don't you have dinner with us at our place?'

'We would like to Michael. Yes, we would love to.'

Somebody else broke into the conversation as I felt the first wave of alcohol come over me. I didn't know what I was saying. I knew I wasn't making much sense, but everybody seemed to laugh and chuckle. Mary came alongside me and I leaned on her for support. She led me over to a chair. I remember talking to somebody, I don't know who. I was feeling dizzy and I was so hot my shirt was wet with sweat. I remember walking out onto the verandah. The night air was cool and refreshing. I could see the lights and the beauty of the harbour. I was on my own, free from the noise. I looked at the boats in the pods, the small jetties. I looked down the line of sailboats, but then I was taken entirely by surprise. There was a beautiful two masted yacht. Her stern rose from the water, curved, and then rose up to a beautiful wooden handrail.

The cockpit appeared quite large; the cabin was a little higher than I would have expected and the windows seemed to be natural timber and complement the cabin. The bow rose up with a beautiful curve to the bow spirit. On the bow there was a sign. I walked over to the handrail on the verandah so I could read it. *My Lady* For Sale, it said. I re-read it. *My Lady* For Sale. I left the verandah and walked down the jetty towards her to re-read the sign. *My Lady* For Sale. There was a small jetty alongside. I stepped onto it and suddenly a man's head appeared out of the cockpit. An elderly man with a grey beard.

His voice boomed. 'Yes, yes, what do you want?'

I was a little surprised. 'I don't know.'

'Well, you had better come aboard.' The old man said.

I was about to step aboard when his voice boomed out again. 'You don't come aboard a vessel like this with your bloody leather shoes. No, get them off!' Nobody had ever spoken to me like that. I slipped my shoes off and stepped aboard. The cockpit looked so comfortable. There were beautiful cushions on the seats, some were leather, some beautifully embroidered fabric. An older lady was sitting on the far side of the cockpit; she nodded to me and continued with her knitting.

'Well boy, you had a better look below, watch out for the bottom step, it's got a little twist to it. Also watch your head on the first beam.'

I was in a beautiful cabin; there was a table with padded seats all around it. The chart table, drawers and cupboards were all secure so that they couldn't move. There was a stove; the maker's name was on the front, Ferris. Cups were hanging on hooks, they were all different colours, and had various seabirds on them with their names printed on them. Everything in the cabin was made from beautifully varnished timber.

'Come and have a look at the rest of the cabin boy.' The word boy annoyed me. I scowled at him as I opened the cabin door. Inside there were four bunks, beautifully painted in yellow. It matched the timber work, there were small cupboards and wardrobes.

On every bunk there was a small compartment for a life-jacket. I turned to my right, or should I say starboard. There was another door. I opened it to find a toilet and a shower, the shower was quite significant for a sailing vessel, but the lady wasn't exactly small. I walked towards the bow and opened the door in front of me.

The old man's voice boomed out again. 'Watch your head on the door frame boy!' It was a little low, but this was probably to give the yacht additional strength. I took a deep breath and let it out slowly, for there in front of me was a beautiful cabin with a double bed, there was plenty of room to move around, with cupboards and drawers and mirrors on the wall. A woman had planned this, not a man. There were lace curtains on the two portholes, it had everything a woman would need. I noticed a small round magnifying mirror sitting on the side table with a pair of fine tweezers. I chuckled to myself, 'Mary would appreciate them.'

I walked back to the cockpit. 'Well, boy, you have seen her now.'

I slowly opened my eyes. My head was pounding, my forehead was tight, my mouth was dry and tasted horrible. I tried to move. My head, my head, my head, dear God, my head. I shut my eyes again hoping the pain might go away. Then my bladder demanded my attention. I didn't know what was worse, my head or my bladder. I had to get up and go to the toilet or my bladder would burst. I threw back the doona knowing I had to lift my head off the pillow. It was like trying to raise a rock. I managed to swing my legs out of bed onto the floor and sit up. I just wanted to die! I don't know how I got into the bathroom. I sat down on the toilet seat because I couldn't stand. To my absolute horror I had not lifted the toilet cover. I tried to stand up quickly before I relieved myself, the pain! When I sat back down I felt pleasure, total pleasure. My body could relax now the pressure had gone. But then I became hot and sweaty. I knew there was a volcano inside my stomach. I spun around and put my head over the toilet bowl and relieved my stomach. Surely no death could be as bad as this; when is it going to end? Every time I thought it was finished, it was back. Finally I was able to stand. I splashed cold water onto my face and washed my hands. Then I saw Mary standing in the doorway with a glass of water and two aspirin.

'Take these aspirin dear, I don't think they can do that much good though. You certainly drank a lot of alcohol last night, but it was your night. You may not remember last night, but you will certainly remember this morning!' She put me back to bed and took the phone off the hook.

Some hours later I opened my eyes. I certainly didn't feel one hundred percent, but I was well enough to put my dressing gown and slippers on and go downstairs. Mary was putting things in boxes and marking what they were in her very efficient way. She smiled at me, 'Feeling better dear?' Her eyes were twinkling, but the expression on her face let me know her amusement and compassion. 'I'll make you some toast and coffee, no milk.' We sat on the verandah in the warm sun. I watched Mary pouring the coffee; my time now belongs to her, she has given me so much support, and I have taken her for granted. She slid my coffee over to me, along with my toast. She reached out and took my hand. 'They certainly gave you a send-off, didn't they dear?'

'Yes, they did. It's a long time since I drank like that and I certainly won't do it again. I wouldn't survive!' My mind went back to the previous night, to the coolness on the verandah. 'I very much appreciated going out onto the verandah dear, to the cool night air, it was just what I needed.' She looked at me puzzled, her head bent slightly to one side. 'I was walking down to the jetty; then I was gliding down the jetty, moving down the jetty, no, that doesn't make sense! I was walking down the jetty; there was a beautiful two masted yacht. I believe they call it a schooner; she was made of timber.' I explained to Mary what she looked like; I described the cockpit, the cabin, the bow, and the windows, the beautiful cushions on the seats. I told her how the old man had said 'watch your head and watch out for the step'. I described the Ferris stove, the mugs on their hooks with the birds on them, the layout of the cabin, the bathroom and sleeping quarters, everything that I had seen. The sign that said *My Lady* For Sale and the old man's voice, 'Get those bloody shoes off.' Mary was staring at me.

'What's wrong dear? Why are you staring at me like that?'

'Well,' she said, 'there is no verandah on the back of the yacht club.'

'But there must be because I was on the verandah I was looking at the boats in their pods, and the air was so crisp and refreshing.'

'John, there isn't a verandah on the yacht club building.'

I sat there staring at her; she is seldom wrong. Over the years she had done a lot of work in the yacht club, raising funds for the club and charities. 'John, you just fell asleep in a chair. You were so drunk that they had to help me put you in the car. Peter from next door helped me put you into bed, you were burning up. I bathed you with cold water and put an ice bag on your head.'

'I think I might go back to bed again dear and sleep this off.'

The next two weeks were spent packing boxes to move to our new home. Now and again I would see Mary stop what she was doing and stare quietly for a few moments. I knew her memories were flooding back. This had been her home; where our children had grown up, celebrated all their birthdays, spent all the happy times of their lives. And the sad times too. I remembered when they all had the measles and the sad times when they had fallen over and hurt themselves. Their growing pains. When they had received various award medals.

I saw Mary pull a tissue from her sleeve and wipe her eyes. 'Everything all right dear?'

'Yes, yes, just the dust in my eyes.' But I knew different.

We moved into our new house and put a lot of the boxes into storage. One morning the phone rang. 'Hello, John.'

'Hello, Frank, how are you?'

'I'm up to my neck in it, got nobody watching my back, but that's not why I rang. The University would like to know whether you could do some lectures on business structure and with that crystal ball of yours, see into the future.'

'Frank, I would love to do some talks.'

'I'll set it up for you John, through the organisation. I believe we are having dinner together next week at Michael's house. It will be like the good old days. See you then, John.'

The receiver clicked. I remembered when I didn't have the time to talk to people; now I've got all the time in the world. 'Mary, could we get out of the house for a while this afternoon. I want to go down to the yacht club.' I didn't know why, I just needed to go there.

'Yes, John. We could get you some new shirts and casual slacks as you're not wearing suits anymore, or ties.'

'That's a good idea. Some new clothes would be good dear.'
I thought about what I had just said; I was starting to relax.

We stopped outside the main security gate to the wharf alongside the yacht club. The security guard recognised us.

'Good afternoon Sir.'

'No, no Malcolm. Those days are gone. It's John and Mary now, we are retired and are free. Can I walk down the wharf Malcolm?'

'Yes, certainly, take your time. If there's anything I can help you with, please ask.'

Mary and I walked down alongside the pods. I stopped abruptly. 'Mary, Mary? There she is, the schooner, just as I'd seen it!' I turned around and looked back at the yacht club. Mary was right; there wasn't a verandah or a handrail. I looked back at Mary; she was reading the name of the yacht; she read it aloud.

'*My Lady*. John, if you were standing up there looking out of the window you would not be able to see the name on this yacht because the sign is in the way.' I froze. Mary had a puzzled look on her face.

'There's got to be a logical reason for this, Mary.' We walked back to the security guard. 'Malcolm, who owns *My Lady*?'

'She's tied up in a legal case. There has been trouble with the owner's will. You know the barrister. Frederick owned all these companies and estates and was always working on behalf of the working man. He died a little while ago. The pod fees have been paid in full for the next five years, and the boat is now tied up in his assets. Frederick loved that boat. He and his wife would take off for two or three months at time. Their children would always be with them during the school holidays. He was a grubby old sod, but I liked him. I always gave him cheek, and he'd give it back. His wife knitted socks for me; they were a great couple.'

'Thank you, Malcolm.'

'Anytime, John, Mary.' He nodded his goodbye.

Mary and I stopped to buy some clothes, but other than that, we didn't say much on the way home.

Over the next two months I did my series of lectures and life seemed to go back into some routine. We both felt a bit lost and agreed that it would take a little time to adjust to this new life. One morning while sitting down to breakfast and reading the newspaper I went to the business section. I was missing being in the business world. Things were happening that I was not involved with, and not making decisions about. I turned to the advertisements; a section of the paper I don't usually read. What did I see but a photo of the schooner *My Lady*. She was part of a liquidation sale of assets. There was a name and number to ring. 'Mary, come and read this.' Mary just put her head to one side.

'That's very interesting, John; I've been thinking about *My Lady*. Why don't you give them a call.'

I rang the number. 'Good morning, my name is John. I have been reading the article about the schooner *My Lady*, is it possible to have a look over her?'

'Yes, Sir. Would 3 pm this afternoon be suitable for you?'

'Yes, it would be. Thank you.'

'Mary, we have an appointment at 3 pm this afternoon.' I will never forget the smile on her face. She disappeared into the bedroom, at 2 pm she reappeared. She was dressed perfectly for the occasion in a white dress, with a light blue trim around the hem, and a white waisted jacket with blue trim on the collar. She wore soft shoes to match.

We soon arrived at the Yacht club. 'Hello. Malcolm.'

'G'day John, Mary. There are two salesmen waiting for you alongside *My Lady*. They have the keys for her.'

'Good Afternoon. My name is John. My wife, Mary.'

'John, Sir.' He shook my hand and nodded to Mary.

'I said my name is John, not Sir.' I laughed.

'Would you care to come aboard John, and I will show you over *My Lady*.'

'Thank you.' Just as the salesman started to step aboard I said, 'Take your blasted shoes off; you don't step on board a vessel like this with leather shoes on!' I don't know why I said it, but I did. Mary just stared at me. I raised my eyebrows and shrugged my shoulders. The salesman stood abruptly for a few moments, then took his shoes off. I did the same.

We were all standing in the cockpit. The agent was trying to find the right key. Finally, he unlocked the door and started to enter the cabin.

'Watch your head and be careful of the step at the bottom; it is slightly twisted,' I said. Again I don't know why I said that.

He looked at me with a surprised look on his face. 'Have you been on this vessel before John?'

I hesitated. 'No, I haven't, but when I first came aboard this vessel, I hit my head and tripped on the bottom step. He was waiting for an answer, but I couldn't give him one. We all went down into the cabin.

Mary burst out laughing. 'John, the mugs with seabirds on all of them, with their names, the table, chart table, cupboards, are all exactly as you said.' She stood there staring, she looked back at me then opened the other door. 'The shower is just as you said it was.' Mary raced forward to the main cabin door.

'Watch your head dear, just watch your head on the door frame.' The salesman was staring at me.

Mary opened the cabin door and put her hands to her mouth. 'John, John, it is absolutely beautiful, just as you explained it, all quite lovely.' Mary gently touched the embroidered cushions. 'They are all so beautiful.'

The salesman told us that all the safety gear is aboard her and a spare generator.

Soon we were back on the jetty. 'If you say that you were never aboard this boat, John, how did you know so much about her?' the salesman asked.

'I can't explain it to you or anybody else, I just know. If you could please email the costing and everything else I should know, I will get back to you.'

'Well John, it is the highest bidder.'

'If you could give me some more information, I'd appreciate it.'

'I'll do that,' he said.

'Thank you.' Mary and I stood there looking at *My Lady*.

The two men walked back up the jetty to the gate, and I saw them briefly talking to Malcolm, then they were gone. 'You like her, don't you Mary?'

'Oh, John, she's absolutely beautiful. I have fallen in love with her.' She looked at me with those big, beautiful pleading eyes. 'Could we, John? Please could we?'

'I will have to play the game dear. I'll put in a bid for her and see what happens.'

As we were walking back up the jetty something made me turn around and look back at *My Lady*, then I heard the old man's voice again, '$300,000 boy, $300,000. Don't waste bloody time.' I shook my head.

Mary was staring at me. 'What's wrong, John? What's wrong?'

'Nothing Mary. Nothing is wrong, just confusing. Let's go home. I have some emails to do and phone calls to make.'

As we walked through the gate, Malcolm chuckled to himself. 'You certainly confused those salesmen, the old man playing his tricks again!'

I stared at him. 'What do you mean by that, Malcolm?'

'Oh, it's just a joke between the old man and myself.' But it was the way he smiled at me. He knew something. But what?

We stopped at the newsagent on the way home where I picked up the latest boats for sale magazines. Once we arrived home I did some figures on our money, and the shares that I thought we could get rid of. I was not in the business world any more to follow them up. I browsed through the magazines but couldn't find any boats like *My Lady*. My feelings were that $300,000 was probably the right price, but I needed to clinch the deal. In my mind's eye I could still see Mary on the jetty, I could still hear her saying 'please John, please'.

I emailed the salesman saying that I would like to put in a bid of $350,000 and pushed the send button. Well, I hope we have just bought a schooner. I walked into the kitchen. 'I have put in a bid for *My Lady*.' Mary ran forward and put her arms around my neck and kissed me.

'John, you really are a softy deep down, aren't you.' She gave me that warm, gentle smile. 'Coffee?'

'Yes, please, dear.' Why do wives always give you that feeling that they have won?

The days went past, and finally I received the email from the estate managers telling me my bid had been accepted, and wanting to know when it would be convenient for me to see them regarding the paperwork.

'Mary come and read this.'

She read it out loud. 'He can see us now John, right now.'

I burst out laughing. 'I have to get all our paperwork together first dear. How about Friday 10 am aboard *My Lady*?'

Mary slowly walked off, singing *I've got you under my skin, no matter what may come, I've got you under my skin, I've got you under my skin.* She gave a little wiggle with her backside.

On Friday we all sat on board *My Lady* and signed the relevant paperwork; Malcolm co-signed for us. We were now the proud owners of *My Lady*. We shook hands with the salesman and his colleague and said goodbye. Mary was ready with a notebook and pencil to write down what she would put where, what this was, and what that was. I saw her doing measurements with her hands. 'I wish I had bought a tape measure, dear,' she said.

'Top drawer on the left.' I don't know what made me say it.

Mary opened the drawer and took out the tape measure. She turned around and looked at me. 'How did you know the tape measure was in there?'

'I don't know dear, I don't know. I seem to know so much about this boat, but I don't know why.'

We spent the next couple of weeks putting what we wanted on her, or should I say what Mary wanted on her. We both did an advanced yachting course on navigation, star reading, wave patterns, weather charts and emergency procedures. There was so much to learn, but we were doing it together. Mary was play-ful, singing to herself all the time. She had become so happy.

Every moment of her day was about *My Lady*. 'Come on dear, get out of bed, we don't have time to sleep in this morn-ing,' or 'Don't sit there in the armchair reading the paper, you've got those things I asked to you do.'

Is this retirement? Nobody told me it was like this when I was the big boss, but now Mary is the big boss, and she loves it. I love it too.

Mary now had everything just as she wanted it. I'd finished my course on electrical equipment aboard the boat.

We had sailed many times around Sydney Harbour and had got to know *My Lady* well. Mary and I had been watching the weather reports, and it appeared the weather was going to be favourable for the following week. 'Mary, how would you like to take *My Lady* up to the Hawkesbury River?'

'Oh John, I've been waiting for you to say something like that. When can we go?'

'Well, there's no reason why we couldn't go tomorrow.' With that Mary disappeared into the bedroom, back out, then into the bathroom, then into the kitchen. She was like a whirlwind, packing things into the car. At 11 pm that night she walked into the office.

John, could we go down to *My Lady* tonight and sleep on board, and leave in the morning?'

I studied her for a few moments. 'Well, well, dear, I don't see any reason why not.'

I chuckled to myself. I don't think she really wants to go! I had better go and get dressed in the appropriate clothes.

We both slept soundly that night onboard *My Lady*. It must have been the gentle movement of the water. It was 10 am before I started the little motor and we left her berth. Malcolm cast off our bow lines. 'We will see you in a couple of days, Malcolm.'

'Enjoy yourselves John, Mary.'

I put the gear stick into reverse, no, that should be astern, and *My Lady* gently moved out of our pod. I turned the wheel, and she swung around to the open harbour. I put the gear stick into neutral, then into forward, she moved gently. Mary came up from the cabin with the cushions. She placed them around the cockpit and disappeared back down and returned with the rest of them. She sat where the elderly lady was sitting when I first came on board.

I pushed the button that said jiff, and the triangular sail on *My Lady's* bow started to unwind and fill with the wind. I pushed the next button which said mainsail, and that sail started to rise and fill with the wind. I gave her a little headway and then turned off the motor.

My Lady gently lay over. I could feel and sense her come alive. I could hear the slop sound of the small waves alongside the boat. 'We are free *My Lady*,' I said.

We tacked back and forth across the harbour avoiding the other yachts, giving way when we had to, we must not take the wind from their sails. If another yacht is crossing your bow at a certain angle, you must give him right of way, but if it is a power boat, he must give you right of way at all times. But don't challenge a Sydney Harbour Ferry or a cruise ship! They are too solid. Soon Sydney Harbour started to disappear behind the headlands and we could see Manly and the Rocks to the entrance.

Mary was standing alongside me in her white dress with the blue trimmings. We could see a big cruise ship coming through the entrance, she looked very majestic, we knew she had the right of way, so we altered course but kept the wind in our sails.

'Can you see the name of that cruise ship Mary?' Mary burst out laughing and then giggled like a little girl.

'Yes, yes, it's the *Queen Mary*. I didn't realise I had a ship named after me.' Mary had such a beautiful smile on her face, she was so happy. As we started to pass the cruise ship, or should I say the cruise ship passed us, some of the passengers on deck were waving. Mary shrieked and waved back, bouncing on her toes with excitement. The number of passengers waving to her was quite extraordinary. Mary couldn't contain herself as she laughed and waved back at them. She nudged me with her shoulder, 'My ship dear, that's my ship'.

'Well, as long as you don't want me to buy it for you dear,' I laughed.

'There's a thought, isn't there?' I nudged her back. 'If you want it dear, I will buy it for you, but only if the price is right.' Mary chuckled to herself 'while you are working out the figures, would you like a cup of coffee?'

'Yes Mary, I would love a cup of coffee.' I pushed the other buttons so that we had all sails up on *My Lady*, and we headed out to sea. Mary came back up with the coffee, and we stood there watching the harbour entrance and the coastline receding. There were many other yachts coming out of the harbour, making this a perfect picture that I knew would stay in my mind forever.

The scenery was so raw and alive, but in another sense, so peaceful, so natural. We stood with the warm sun on our backs and admired the majestic view. As we went further out to sea, we took in more of the beautiful coastline. I'd only ever seen it from a plane, but the perspective from the boat was more majestic that I could have imagined.

The colours of the surf, white spray, blue and green water glistening in the sunlight, silver gold, yellow, it was a painter's dream. The birds were flying high in the sky then closing their wings and diving into the water to catch fish. A pod of dolphins were playing in the surf. Mary took my hand and leaned into my side. It was just the two of us and we enjoyed the solitude together.

By now we had passed most of the other yachts and were out into the open sea. I had already worked out our course and set the automatic pilot for the Hawkesbury River. *My Lady* seemed to be at total peace with herself, the wind in her sails, she was leaning over slightly to one side, gracefully rising up to meet the swell.

Mary's voice rose from the cabin. 'Scotch and dry dear?'

'Yes, Mary, that would be good.' As I watched the bow my mind was at peace. I hadn't felt this way for a very long time, there were no problems or politics, just Mary and me.

I knew, or sensed, Mary was coming up out of the cabin, I didn't look around. 'Your Scotch and dry dear.'

'Thank you, Mary.' I reached out my hand and took the drink, then I glanced in her direction and nearly dropped my drink. I was totally surprised, but pleasantly. Mary's hair was hanging loose around her shoulders. She had no clothes on, not a stitch! She giggled and went to the back of the cockpit and lay down on the cushions. I had never seen Mary do anything like this before.

'John, for the first time in our marriage I feel that I am free. It's just you and me.' She closed her eyes, and I knew the movement of *My Lady* gently rocked her into a deep sleep, something she had needed for a long time. Mary only slept for three or four hours a night, she couldn't sleep any longer. She never slept in the afternoons, but here she was, looking absolutely beautiful. My Mary, totally at peace with herself. I put the boat into automatic pilot, got my scotch and dry and sat down, gently lifted her legs and put them on my lap. As I looked at her the words of a song came into my mind.

I sat there peacefully enjoying the magic moment, looking at Mary, thinking of how beautiful she was, of how much she had given me over the years, and how much she had wanted to buy this beautiful schooner. Now it was just the two of us. I no longer belonged to the company; I was hers.

Time drifted by so quickly and soon we were near the entrance to the Hawkesbury River. Some other yachts were coming a bit too close considering what Mary had on! I gently placed my hand on her foot and softly rubbed it with my hand; she opened her eyes and smiled at me. 'Mary, we are getting close to the mouth of the Hawkesbury River, and some yachts are coming a bit too close.' The smile on her face changed as she realised how she looked.

'Oh my god John!' she sprung to her feet, crouched down and headed for the cabin. I laughed, and she shouted out, 'Don't you bloody laugh John, it's not funny.' Watching her crouched down with no clothes on trying to get to the cabin quickly, was to me, very amusing.

Ten minutes later she emerged from the cabin wearing a T-shirt and a pair of shorts. She was carrying two cups of coffee and some sandwiches. We could see waves crashing on the beach, seagulls were flying high, dipping and diving, swirling and flying back high. Seabirds were diving on the surface of the water catching fish. Other yachts were also entering the mouth of the Hawkesbury River, along with a few powerboats and fishing boats. I watched a boat called *Bounty* sail through the entrance, she was a majestic craft in full sail, glistening white in the sunlight.

We turned to our port side where there was safe anchorage. *Bounty* was anchoring there along with a few other yachts. There were houses dotted on the hill. We could see people on the beach, some walking dogs and others playing with their children. It was a very peaceful scene.

I stowed away all our sails, started the little motor and found a safe place to anchor. Mary pulled the little lever back on the anchor winch. It clattered as it went out, then stopped as the anchor hit the bottom. I eased the little motor into stern, *My Lady* chuffed back and some more anchor chain ran out. I put the motor into neutral and shouted, 'Right Mary'. She put the lever back into the lock position. I eased the gear lever into a stern and felt the anchor bite, then put the little motor back into neutral and turned it off.

I watched Mary as she came into the cockpit. Seeing her with her hair down, in loose comfortable clothes without shoes, gave me a warm feeling. How had I missed something so important? I had not taken the time to stop and smell the roses. But now I could. I could see Mary, and I could be with Mary, we could be together, as one.

'Would you like a drink, John?' Mary asked.

'Yes please, Mary.'

She came out of the cabin with a bottle of good wine and two glasses. We sat in the cockpit and I listened to her talking and giggling. Mary hadn't talked like this for many years. I felt like I had gone back in time.

'Would a light tea be all right John, maybe chicken and salad?'

'Yes Mary.'

She stood up, then knelt in front of me, and put her head on my lap. 'John, it's been absolutely beautiful today, I've had a marvellous day. I do love you. I think I love you more now than I ever did, you are now my John.' She giggled and kissed me on the end of my nose. 'You are my slave forever!'

I gave her the royal wave. 'Anything you desire my lady, I am your genie in the yacht!' She giggled and disappeared into the cabin.

I poured the rest of the wine into my glass and sat watching the darkness creep across the water. The lights on the shore were starting to twinkle and yachts were turning on their cabin lights. I could hear laughter and faint conversations. The people on the *Bounty* were singing and laughing. This experience was something not heard or seen in the city. It was magic. I had so much to be grateful for.

Mary called out to me 'John, tea is ready.' I stood up and took a good look around me, then I heard him, in that deep throaty voice, chuckling, 'well boy, what do you think now?'

For a moment, I froze. 'John, tea is ready!' Mary called out again. I shook myself and went below. We drank another bottle of wine with our dinner. We were tired and didn't talk much during dinner.

'It's been a long day, could we have an early night dear?'

'Yes Mary, I think that would do both of us the world of good.' I went back on deck to check the navigational and mast lights, but I know that I was actually listening for the old man. He had gone. I went down below, had a quick shower and crawled into bed alongside Mary and fell into a deep sleep.

The next morning I woke to sunlight streaming through the porthole window. Mary was huddled tightly into my shoulder, my arm was cradling her neck, she didn't normally sleep like this. She usually stayed on her side of the bed, not wanting to wake me when she got up during the night. Not wanting to move in case I woke her, I enjoyed this magical moment. Unfortunately my mind started to go back into work mode. I was wondering if we had dragged the anchor during the night? Where were the other yachts? What is the wind doing? There was no sound from the other yachts' rigging. I moved slightly and Mary woke up. She giggled, 'Who is this strange man I'm with? You are so big, strong and handsome. You could have your way with me anytime you wish!' She giggled again.

'Well Mary, there is somewhere I have to go first.' I got up and went to the toilet then went up on deck. We were still anchored in the same place, there was no wind, the water was calm. I heard the noise of an anchor chain and looked around to see the *Bounty*. She was about to leave and was lifting her anchor, her topsails had already been set, trying to catch any high breezes; most of the other yachts had already gone. I looked at the ship's clock, 9:30 am, and grinned to myself. I don't have to be anywhere, I don't really have anything I have to do. Then I chuckled to myself, yes, I do! I went back down below.

At 11 am Mary was cooking eggs and bacon and singing to herself. 'Whatever Lola wants, Lola gets…'

Just then my mobile phone rang. What sod would be ring-ing me now? I don't want to talk to anybody. Mary answered it and handed it to me.

'John here.'

The voice came back. 'Yes John, Terry here.'

'Yes Terry, how can I help you?'

'I've been trying to get in touch with you, but your phone was out of service, where are you?'

'At the mouth of the Hawkesbury River.'

'Every time I ring you I think about retirement and not having to deal with the Board of Directors! The University wants you back for a series of talks. Can you do it?'

I looked over at Mary and looked into her eyes, then shrugged my shoulders. 'Yes Terry. I will phone you when we get back.'

'Thank you, John. Talk to you later.'

Mary put a hand on my shoulder as she put a plate of bacon and eggs in front of me. 'Could we stay here a bit longer John?'

'I don't see why not Mary, the time is ours.'

We spent the next two days talking, sipping wine, reading our books, resting or sleeping. Time finally caught up with us. Our children were coming back from Singapore and Mary had promised them we would meet them at the airport. I knew that in the next couple of days the weather would be changing and we needed to set sail before it did.

At 8 am the next morning, Mary brought breakfast up to the cockpit, and we sat there looking around us.

'John, when the children are home it's going to be very noisy and I don't really think the house is big enough for two women. Could we maybe live on *My Lady*? There is certainly enough room for just the two of us.' I thought about it for a few moments.

'I can't really see any reason why not dear; we have every-thing we need aboard.' She threw her arms around my neck; my coffee nearly went flying off the table. 'Steady dear, you will choke me to death, and then I won't be able to eat my bacon and eggs, and that would be a waste.' Mary just laughed and gave me her cheeky grin.

'I will get you another cup of coffee my darling.' With that she disappeared below. Soon her head popped out of the hatchway. 'Do you think the University would appreciate you doing a talk about retirement and sailing around the globe with not a care in the world?'

'Mary, I can do a talk on that any day, but I don't think I'd be asked back to the University again.' Mary burst out laughing.

'Then I think that's the right lecture for you to do!' She disappeared below again.

After we drank our coffee Mary picked up the dishes and went down into the galley. I checked all the instruments, checked the batteries had power, checked the fuel, water, fresh drinking water and started the motor. I saw the gauge starting to rise, it was recharging the batteries. I pushed the throttle lever to give the engine a little bit more speed, and the AMP gauge rose a bit more, it was in the yellow mark then it clicked into the green. Mary went forward to the anchor winch and was watching me.

'Hold on Mary, we're going forward.' I put the gear lever into forward then back to neutral. 'Right Mary.' She released the lever to unlock the anchor winch, then I switched the anchor winch to up. The chain started to clatter as it wound up and slowly disappeared into its socket. 'Right Mary,' I said as I switched it off. She put the lever back into the lock.

My Lady started to swing with the tide. We set all sails again and were on our way. Mary stood at the stern thoughtfully watching where we had spent the last couple of magical days. We headed back out to sea. There was a little bit more of a breeze than when we had entered the Hawkesbury so we stayed close to the shoreline, as we headed back to Sydney. I knew the breeze would be much stronger if we went further out. We were now heading for home.

My Lady seemed to rise and fall with the swells, heaving to one side with the wind in her sails, a gentle rhythm. Mary stood alongside me, her arm entwined in mine, her head on my shoulder. Suddenly, we were surrounded by a pod of dolphins, they were on both sides of our bow, swimming backwards and forwards, just under the surface, others were leaping out of the water, splashing back and disappearing. They seemed to be playing a game, standing up on their tails and going backwards on the surface of the sea, then dropping back into the water. They seemed to be talking to each other, with clicking and squawking sounds, like children playing in the park.

Mary rose up on the balls of her feet, laughing and giggling, pointing at this one and that. We didn't want this magic moment to end. The sun was warm on our skin; I watched Mary's hair being blown about in the gentle breeze. I was full of joy. Mary was mine, she had always been mine, but I had never seen her like this before, and I was enjoying every single moment of it. We watched the waves once again crashing onto the rocks, they were white and majestic. The cliffs rose high into the air, seagulls and other birds were feeding in the water. There were small fishing boats, some with just one man in them, others with their families. All of a sudden Mary shrieked.

'Whales John!' She could see the waterspouts rising high into the air. Mary disappeared below, and then came back with the binoculars. 'John, did you see that tail rising out of the water? Did you see that splash? They must be huge.'

'Mary, could I look through the binoculars please?' She giggled, wiggled her backside and laughed again.

'No, no John, they're mine!' she said in a mocking voice and giggled again. She was so happy; I gave her a wicked chuckle.

'Then you will pay for that tonight my dear!'

'Oh, you wicked man; you will be gentle with me, won't you?' I gave her one of those looks, she giggled again. Mary handed me the binoculars. Time just seemed to disappear and soon we arrived at The Heads, heading into Sydney Harbour. We stood looking at the beauty of the harbour. We didn't talk, we just watched. There were no words to describe it.

'John, could we anchor in Manly tonight and go back to the pod in the morning?'

'Yes Mary, that'd be a good idea.' Manly is a good anchorage just inside Sydney heads to the starboard, or to the right. We anchored for the night. Mary cooked a good supper and we sat in the cockpit talking about our little adventure and how much we had enjoyed it. Then my phone started to ring. 'I thought I'd switched that damn thing off,' I said.

'You had John, but I thought I had better turn it back on.'

I went down into the cabin, annoyed and frustrated that our special moment had come to an end. I picked up the phone, 'Yes, what do you want?'

'Dad, where the hell are you? We've been worried, you both have become like children! Could you please put Mum on the phone?'

'Just a minute.' I climbed up the steps to the cockpit, thinking to myself 'you never used to ring us from Singapore did you'.

'It's our daughter dear, she wants you.' Mary gave me the look that she didn't want to talk to anyone. I'd never seen her look like that before.

'Yes dear, what do you want?' All I could hear was Mary's voice, 'yes dear, no dear, yes dear.' Then, 'Yes we could. Daddy is doing some lectures, we could do it then. She wants Ugg boots? A bit hot for them, isn't it? Yes she's at that age. See you tomorrow afternoon dear, bye, love you.' Mary looked at me, 'She says goodbye dear.' I waved.

The next morning I woke up at seven-thirty. Mary was cuddled tight into my arms and still asleep. I could hear other boats moving about us. Then I heard somebody knocking on the cabin. I whispered 'Mary' and she opened her eyes. 'I think there is somebody on board Mary, I'm going up on deck to see.' I opened the cabin door and peered out.

A voice said 'Good Morning Sir. We apologise for waking you so early.' The man was dressed in a Harbour Trust Police Uniform. I went up into the cockpit.

'Yes Officer, how can I help you?'

'Are you the owner of this vessel?'

'Yes Sir, I am.'

'And your name Sir?'

'I am John Henderson.'

'You came into the harbour late yesterday evening?'

'Yes, we did.'

'Where did you come from Sir?'

'We sailed up to the Hawkesbury River three days ago and have just returned.'

'And where are you going now?'

'Back to our pod at the yacht club.'

He smiled at me. 'Now I know this schooner. I couldn't remember where I had seen her before. You would have had a good trip'

'Yes we did.'

'Sorry to have disturbed you Sir, we have to check all vessels coming into the harbour.' Mary's head appeared out of the cabin. 'Sorry to have disturbed you Madam.'

Mary gave him a cheeky smile. 'You never know who you are going to meet do you Michael?' The officer's head went back slightly, and he stood straight. He stared at Mary for a few moments, and then burst out laughing.

'Mary, I didn't recognise you. You look quite normal. Oh, I didn't mean it like that.'

'I perfectly understand Michael. *My Lady* has changed me quite a bit.'

Michael chuckled again. 'Mum won't believe me.'

'John, Michael's mother and I belong to the same ladies club.'

'It pays to have friends in the right place.' I winked at her and she grinned back. I put my hand out and shook Michael's.

'There's no paperwork to do John. Good Morning to you both.' He stepped off our boat onto his vessel and they took off at high speed.

'Well Mary, it shows our people are on the ball. He thinks you're quite normal, that's a nice compliment.'

'John, don't say anymore, I can see what you're thinking.' She slapped me on the shoulder.'

'I wasn't going to say anything dear; I was just going to save it till later.'

'Well John, I would appreciate it if you'd have a shave before we got back.'

'Yes dear, yes. Back to normal.'

We slowly eased *My Lady* into her pod, Malcolm was there waiting. He secured our bow lines. 'Hello John, Mary.'

'Hello Malcolm.' I stepped onto the jetty. There wasn't any movement under my feet and it felt wrong. I shook Malcolm's hand. 'Malcolm, Mary and I have to go to the airport to pick up the children, they're coming back from Singapore. We will be staying on board *My Lady*. I wonder whether you could fuel her up for us?'

'Yes John, certainly. Here are the keys to your car, it's in bay number six. There are gates in front of it, I've unlocked them.'

'Why did you move the car Malcolm?'

'There were three men looking at the car and I didn't like the look of them. They were well dressed, but I just didn't like them.'

'Thank you, Malcolm, thank you. Oh Malcolm, I didn't mean the children are coming back here, just Mary and myself. We are going to live on board.'

He grinned at me.

'Yes Malcolm, we think you need somebody to have coffee with every now and then.

'I look forward to that John.'

We picked our family up from the airport and they did not stop talking all the way home. We told them we were going to be living on board the yacht. The look on their faces left us a little confused. We didn't know what they were thinking or what they had in store for us. Had we spoiled their plans? Who knows.

I gave the two lectures that Terry called me about while we were away. They went very well and I was paid handsomely.

One morning soon after, Mary and I were having break-fast in the cabin when my phone rang 'Yes John here,' I answered.

'Hello John, it's Terry.'

'Yes Terry, how can I help you?'

'Are you interested in some more lectures?' I saw Mary's eyes widen as she shook her head from side to side.

'We're going to be busy for the next three months, Terry. The weather is going to be quite good and we're going to go up the coast towards Cairns and have a look around.'

Mary stood up, she had a beautiful smile on her face. I could see the sun radiating out of that smile. She moved around the table and put her arms around my neck and nibbled my ear, then said into my phone, 'Terry, he is mine for the next three months; you can't have him, sorry.'

'Mary, I perfectly understand, see you when you get back.' Terry burst out laughing. 'You lucky pair, bitch, bitch, bitch. Have fun you two, have fun.'

Mary rubbed her fingers through my hair and messed it all up, then disappeared to the bow with pencil and paper in hand. 'John, how many toilet rolls do you think we'll need for three months, and toothpaste? Oh, I think I better get some more toothbrushes and toiletries. What else are we going to need?'

I couldn't get in a word edgeways, her mind was racing forwards. I started to move to get up to do what I had to do. 'John don't get up, I need help.'

'Yes dear.' She disappeared again, came back up, then she was gone again. Michael said she was normal, what is normal for a woman? I wondered. Is it panic because she's not prepared? Then they're happiest when they are like that and giving men orders. I'll just wait here and see what comes next.

'John, don't just sit there, we've got things to do!'

'Yes Mary, I'll get busy. I'll just go and check the paper-work with Malcolm.'

'That's a good idea John.'

I walked into Malcolm's small office. 'Have you got a cup of coffee, Malcolm? I need it!'

'What have you done John?'

'I told Mary we are going away for three months.'

'And now you're staying out of her way John?'

'Yes, I am.' Malcolm and I drank coffee and talked for an hour or so. When I went back to Mary she was sitting at the table writing on her notepad. Before she could say a word I said 'Mary, I got it all sorted out, everything is in order, things are in place. Malcolm knows what's to be done and we can rely on him.' She didn't even glance up.

'Yes dear, that's good.' She went on with what she was doing.

'Do you want me to bring the car around Mary?'

'Yes dear, I'm going on my own. You will only buy what we don't really need, ice-cream, strawberry topping, liquorice allsorts. We've only got so much room onboard.'

'Mary, let me buy the alcohol.' She looked up at me, and then went back to her shopping list. 'I'll get the car.'

As I started to leave her voice followed me. 'Could you take your golf clubs and your bowling ball out of the boot. I need all the space I can get.'

'Yes dear.' I remembered when people used to say that to me, *yes sir, certainly sir, straight away sir, I'm on my way, sir.* What happened? I had a warm feeling in my body, like when you take the first sip of scotch and dry.

The next morning at six, Malcolm was letting the bowlines go, and we were on our way. Once again, we were heading to the entrance of Sydney Harbour. Mary was down below cooking breakfast; I could smell the bacon. Looking over the bow, my thoughts were everywhere, but nowhere. I was relaxed. I was suddenly startled by his voice. 'Well boy, you are finally doing it. She is going to show you a lifestyle you always wanted. Fair winds to you boy, fair winds.' I spun around looking for him, but there was nobody there. I thought I saw a depression in the cushion on the far side of the cockpit.

Mary came up with two egg and bacon sandwiches and two mugs of coffee. She stood staring at the scenery. I reached out and took my sandwich and coffee, the egg was dripping out of the sandwich.

Mary turned to face me. 'Oh, John, this view is so beautiful.'

'Yes Mary, I know exactly what you're saying.' We leant against each other for support as *My Lady* gently eased back and forth with the swell. We ate our sandwiches and drank our coffee.

'John, I don't know what you will think of this, but when I was cooking our breakfast I was just about to put some oil in the pan, and a woman's voice said to me *don't put that oil in the frying pan dear, your eggs will slop around, just put the eggs straight in.* I turned around, but there wasn't anyone there!'

'Yes, Mary, I understand perfectly. I think it's something we are going to have to live with, they are still aboard this vessel, the vessel is their spirit. Mary, I've been looking closely at the charts that were left on board, the old man had put pencil marks and crosses indicating where to anchor, the time it takes to sail from A to B. If you take your time reading the abbreviations he had written in pencil, they are full of information. It's as if he'd deliberately left it there for us. So Mary, I will take his advice. This is going to be a very interesting voyage!'

'John, could we anchor in the Hawkesbury River tonight?'

'Of course Mary. We're in no hurry to go anywhere.'

Once again we were in the mouth of the Hawkesbury River. Mary was on the bow by the anchor winch. We worked together as a team, we didn't have to say anything, just a nod or a gesture. Everything seemed to happen naturally; we had become part of *My Lady*. We sat quietly in the cockpit as we ate supper and drank our wine.

We were on our way the next morning at six. We had a good steady breeze and there were three other yachts taking the same course as us. We all gave each other a small wave of acknowledgement. Mary went below and I could hear her talking to the other women on the radio. It always amazed me the way women could connect with each other. Mary came back to the cockpit with coffee and we chatted about her new-found friends.

'John, what is that over there? Something white with a yellow ball beside it.'

'I don't know dear, could you please get the binoculars.'

Mary started to climb down into the cabin. 'Mary, could you please get the ones that are in the front cabin, bottom drawer.'

'Those big clumsy ones?'

'Yes, please.'

Mary came back into the cockpit and handed me the big binoculars 'These are so big and clumsy, and they look terrible.'

'The old man would have kept these for a reason. You keep changing the settings on those other ones to suit yourself, so I will keep using these.' I lifted the big old binoculars to my eyes and I got a big surprise. Do I tell Mary these are far better than hers? I chuckled, not yet. 'There's a pelican and a yellow buoy.

'What are they doing?' Mary asked.

'I don't know.' I replied.

'John, could we go over there and have a look.'

'Yes Ma'am!' I turned the wheel slightly to starboard so that we still had the wind in our sails. I laughed as I watched Mary walk back and forth trying to get a better look and getting frustrated.

'John, can you get closer?'

'Yes, Ma'am.' She gave me a sharp look as I saluted her. 'Mary, could you get me the boat hook, it's clipped on the side of the seat. A long pole with a hook on one end of it.'

'What do you want that for John? You can't hook a pelican with that!'

'There seems to be a lot of fishing line around the pelican.' I turned the vessel into the wind, and the sails went slack. I took the boat hook from Mary and reached out and caught the fishing line in the boat hook and pulled it closer to the boat. 'Mary see if you can reach over to the pelican, then I can pull the line in.'

'Will it bite me?' Mary said hesitantly.

'I don't know, but it looks too weak even to lift its head.' Mary reached over the side. I held the boat hook tight in my right hand and reached out and took a handful of Mary's T-shirt in the other hand, just in case.

'John, are pelicans heavy?'

'I wouldn't think so dear.'

Mary soon had the pelican by its neck and pulled it closer in. She grabbed its tail feathers in one hand and lifted it out of the water onto the side of the boat. I pulled the tangle of fishing line and rope into the cockpit. Mary had changed her position, she sat down on the seat and was cuddling the pelican. Then the orders started coming in.

'John, what does a pelican drink, fresh or sea water?'

'I don't really know dear.'

'Get some towels and a knife to cut this line off the pelican.'

'Yes dear, yes, but first of all, I'll get the yacht back on course.' I turned *My Lady* back into the wind and her sails filled with wind. I then pressed the automatic pilot button. We cut the fishing line off the pelican. It was a very strong line. The pelican was still alive but very weak. The yellow buoy had about 20 foot of rope tied to it. It looked like it had been cut with a propeller, fishing line and rope had got tangled up together somehow, and the poor pelican had got itself tangled up as well. The pelican now had its head resting in Mary's armpit. It gave an occasional little croak as Mary stroked it down with a towel. Tears were trickling down Mary's cheeks.

'Oh, you poor little dear, you are safe now, you are safe.' She cuddled the pelican with so much affection and tenderness that tears started to form in my eyes. Were they for Mary or were they for the pelican? I shook my head. I never used to blubber like this. If the board could see me now! What would they say? I went below and made us a drink.

Mary's voice boomed out 'Could you please bring two tins of sardines and one tin of pilchards with you. They are where the sugar is kept.'

I came up into the cockpit with the drinks and tins of fish. 'I think this pelican must be hungry. Could you open the tins please John.'

I put two tins and Mary's drink on the little table and went to have a sip of mine. Mary spoke in a warm compassionate voice, 'John, the pelican is starving, could you please open the tins.'

'Yes, dear.' I took off the keys for the sardines and opened them.

'John, how would you feed a pelican?'

'I suppose you would open its beak and put the food into the pouch.' I handed Mary one of the tins and with two hands opened the pelican's beak, it didn't seem to worry. Mary emptied one tin in, then the other two tins. I let the pelican close its beak and took a sip of my drink. Nothing seemed to happen, the pelican just sat there in Mary's arms. Mary looked at me with those sad eyes. Then, the pelican opened its eyes and lifted its beak into the air; we saw its throat swell up and knew that the food had gone down its throat, then its big head settled down into its chest. Mary started to cry again, speaking softly she said, 'It's going to be alright, the pelican is going to live.' She gently cuddled the pelican and the pelican seemed to lean into her.

'Why don't you have your drink and sit with your pelican, I will make us something to eat,' I said.

'Thanks John. There are rolls in the bread bin, and some ham, cheese and salad in the fridge.'

I'd never seen this side of Mary before. *My Lady* seems to bring out the best in her, and I am enjoying every moment of it.

Mary sat there stroking the pelican. I remember I used to give Mary commands. Do this, do that, don't forget this or that, could you arrange this for me, meet me for lunch, we have a dinner party tonight, could you be ready with my suit. Many small things that I needed to survive in the corporate world, that were so important to me. Sometimes she would raise her eyebrows at me and I knew that I'd gone too far, or she would suggest this or that. I would frown at her and say no dear, or slightly raise my shoulders and say whatever you think is right dear. But now, Mary is giving the commands, and I seemed to be enjoying it. Mary sat for about an hour, stroking the pelican and talking to it. What had happened to me, sitting here with Mary and the pelican, with *My Lady*, watching the beauty of her white sails, the gentle way she would rise and fall to meet the gentle waves. I felt totally relaxed, I would have trouble sitting for an hour doing nothing, thinking nothing, no, that is wrong, I am thinking, but of totally different things now. I could see Mary starting to fidget and move, I wonder what's going through her mind now?

"John could you watch the pelican for a few minutes while I go below?"

"Yes dear, not a problem."

I just took for granted where she was going, but then I heard a voice on the radio, she couldn't wait to let the other women know about the pelican, it was constant chatter. I wonder what their husbands thought, listening to all the chatter? Good God! Women can talk! At one stage I thought the tears of the women were going to come through the radio, but as Mary would say, 'that's you, you have a funny imagination'. I heard her ask the women *does a pelican drink fresh or sea water?* I thought to myself, I would say both. A short time later Mary came up with 2 cups of coffee and a glass of water. At least I assumed it was water. Mary handed me my cup and sat hers down on the little sidetable. She knelt down in front of the pelican and gently opened its beak and poured a little of the water into its beak, then gently closed it, the pelican lifted it beak into the air, then swallowed the water, it made a noise like a croak, then its eyes opened wide, it seemed to be looking straight at Mary. I would swear it smiled, it gave another croak and settled back down. I looked at Mary, puzzled, 'What did you put in that water?'

Mary replied with a smile 'A tablespoon of brandy. My grandmother once told me her favourite rooster fell into the well and it was a very cold and wet day. She retrieved the rooster and dried it with a towel. Then she placed him in the wood oven to dry him off, she also gave him a teaspoon of brandy. She said that her and her husband couldn't stop laughing at the funny noises he was making. He lived for another five happy, healthy years. If it's good enough for my grandmother's rooster, then it's good enough for my pelican.' Mary picked up the pelican, sat down, put him on her lap and gently stroked him, saying 'you'll be alright my darling, I'm going to take care of you, I've never had a pet of my own, I do have John though!' John shook his head and went to check the sails.

That night after following the pencilled instructions on the chart, we anchored in Nelson's Bay. The following day we were at Tyree, then Port Macquarie, Coffs Harbour, Evans Head then Coolangatta. Mary had been in touch with the other yachts for the whole trip. We were all taking the same journey. 'Mary, we could go inside to Stradbroke Island and Brisbane or go out to sea and the South Pacific Ocean.' Mary studied the charts with me.

'Would we motor John, or sail inside?'

'I think we could sail. See these marks in pencil on the chart, he has given us lots of information, there's warnings about the strong tides. He said we can go in under sail if we are with the tide, but if we are going against the tide he suggested using the motor. I checked the tides with the coast guard and all seemed well enough to sail in.'

Mary gently patted me on the backside. 'John, you know that women are really in command don't you!'

I grinned, 'I will sort that out later.'

Mary gave a chuckle 'We'll see John, we'll see.'

There's nothing worse than a wife who is psychic! Mary was back on the radio, chatting away and looking back on the chart in deep discussion with another couple of women who joined in the conversation. I shook my head. I thought I was alone with you Mary, that I had you all to myself. That was just a myth, wasn't it.

Mary glanced up at me from the radio. 'What was that dear?' Then she said, 'Coffee would be nice dear.'

That night the other three yachts anchored nearby and their crew came aboard *My Lady*. We drank wine and ate nibbles until the early hours of the morning. All the women fell in love with the pelican, but they wouldn't touch it. The pelican changed its resting place to the top of the deck where it obviously felt safe. Later on it moved to the bow.

Time didn't matter. We all watched the sun rise, nobody needed to say anything, everyone enjoyed the moment. We had agreed to sail together further up the coast. It gave us all a sense of security staying together, or was it companionship? Either way, we enjoyed each other's company. We all agreed we didn't need to go into Brisbane, instead we went to Moreton Island and stayed there for a couple of days.

It was there, early one morning that the pelican spread his wings, flapped them up and down, turned and looked at us for a few minutes, and the next moment he was in the air and free. Mary clung onto my arm, tears were pouring down her cheeks. I felt a little sad too, but I was very proud of Mary for nursing the pelican back to good health.

We left Morton Island and headed to Caloundra, then on to Noosa Heads where we stayed for a couple of days. While there we bought more provisions and wine; no, no, we bought more wine than provisions! When we left Noosa Heads we sailed to Fraser Island which was so beautiful, we stayed for a week.

While spending so much time on *My Lady,* there were many things we started to notice that didn't quite make sense. The bench in the galley went right up to the bulkhead, but the cupboard stopped 30 centimetres short of the bulkhead. I kneeled down and peered into the cupboard and noticed the side of the cupboard also stopped 30 centimetres short. Why would they do that? These cupboards were built for the yacht.

While I was laying on the bed in the master cabin looking towards the stern I wondered why the door to the cabin had been made so heavy? Was it to support the mast? I doubted that, it was too heavy. The door had been beautifully carved with birds and fish, but the carvings were separated from each other in panels.

The beams in the galley which the cups were hanging on seemed to be way too big, way out of proportion. Was it just my imagination, or was I asking too many questions?

From Fraser Island we headed up to Bundaberg, then on to Gladstone; how it had changed over the years. I remember when I first went there it was just a muddy creek, and the cannery had closed down. Back then the town had four women to one man because most of the men had left looking for work. It was a single man's daydream, but at the same time, very dangerous.

'Mary, do you remember Peter Brooks?'

'Yes dear, he lives around here, doesn't he?'

'Well, last time I spoke with him, yes.'

Mary went and checked the computer, found his phone number, and gave him a call.

'Good Morning Peter, it's Mary and John here.'

'Good God, where are you? Peter asked, 'I haven't seen you for such a long time!'

'We're in Gladstone, Peter.'

'Where in Gladstone are you, Mary?'

'We are tied up at a small wharf.' There was silence on the phone for a few moments.

'You say you are tied up at a small wharf?' Peter asked, sounding very confused.

'Yes Peter, we have our own yacht!' Mary laughingly replied.

'This I've got to see. Give me the name of the jetty. Hang on, wait a minute while I get a pencil.' Mary gave Peter the name of the jetty. Half an hour later Peter and his wife were there.

I shouted, 'Come on board, Peter, come on board, and take those blasted shoes off. You don't come aboard with those shoes on!' The words rushed out of my mouth before I realised what I was saying.

Peter looked at me startled. He burst out laughing. 'You haven't changed a bit, still in command John, still in command.'

I knew Mary's eyes were staring at me, but she stepped in and said. 'He may have been Peter, but now he's gained a sense of humour as well.'

'Yes, Mary, I quite understand that now John doesn't have the weight of the company on his shoulders, he can be himself.'

As Mary and Peter's wife, Chris, went into the galley to prepare a meal, Peter put a hand on my shoulder. 'The man you prepared to take the helm is doing an excellent job. That contract the sleazy lawyer friend of ours had put together,' Peter chuckled, 'with his hairpiece over his eyes, did not get his own way. You certainly picked the right man for the job John.'

Mary and Chris soon appeared with the meal. They were happily chatting.

'Peter, come and have a look down below and let the women chat. We talked about the company, about *My Lady* and where we were headed.

'John, have you been out to the swaying reef yet?' Peter asked.

'No Peter, we haven't.'

'Then let me take you out there tomorrow, I have a boat with a nice big motor and it needs a good run. Will eight o'clock be okay with you both?'

'Thanks, Peter. I think we'd enjoy that.'

The next morning I was hanging onto the rail as Peter's high-speed boat was racing through the water at 28 knots. Mary and Chris were sitting on the stern, their hair blowing about in the wind. They were both laughing and shrieking with joy.

Chris shouted out, 'I am so enjoying this Mary. I wish we could go faster!'

I saw Peter push the accelerator just a little bit further. I don't know what speed we were going, but the spray from the stern rose high into the air. I looking towards the bow the boat seemed to be just gliding through the water. Suddenly Peter put it into a left turn and the boat slightly eased to one side. I could feel the stern sliding into the water; the women shrieked even louder. I held on for dear life! Peter turned the boat into the opposite direction, the women shrieked again. Mary was laughing loudly.

Peter put the boat back on course. What amused Peter and me most was the two women were wearing cotton blouses and they were soaked through. I looked at Peter and he winked at me. Mary shouted to Peter to do it again. Peter looked at me and I shrugged my shoulders. He grinned and looked around to make sure everything was clear and then turned the boat, this time with a tighter turn, then back in the opposite direction with a tighter turn again. Spray rose everywhere, I could feel the back of the boat trying to slide into the water. Then Peter turned the boat back onto its original course and eased back the throttle.

'John, what we like about this boat is that we can be children again and it doesn't interfere with anybody. The business world we live in is a nightmare and it's getting worse but here we can let steam go.' Peter looked back at the two women with a smile on his face and winked at me again. It was one of those magical days. We felt invigorated. Peter handed me a beer from the icebox. Chris and Mary had already opened their bottle of white wine.

Peter looked at me. 'John, there is a seafood restaurant at the wharf, can we buy you a meal? The crabs are beautiful.'

'I've never turned down a free meal.' Peter laughed out loud, picked up his mobile phone and rang for a reservation.

'Do you think the women are dressed appropriately?' he winked.

'The answer is yes, although somehow I don't think the women would think so.' I nudged Peter. 'Ladies, Peter suggests we have a seafood meal. If we go straight there would that be alright with you?'

Mary gave me that look. She reached across the seat, picked up two towels and handed one to Chris. They wrapped the towels around their blouses.

'John, you have such a wonderful personality, and you are so funny.' Chris looked at Mary and said, 'Mary, we will sort them out later!' They shook hands.

Peter nudged me 'Trouble on the horizon boss, trouble on the horizon.'

The next morning it was windy and raining so we decided to stay in Gladstone. We hired a car and drove to Longreach, stayed overnight and drove back the next day. After five enjoyable days we sailed to Mackay, then onto Townsville and Cairns.

'We should start thinking about heading home.' I said to Mary one morning. The weather will start to change in the next month, and if we leave soon we'll have time to stop off at a few of the islands we passed on the way up.'

'Okay John.' Mary had a sad look in her eyes, but then she smiled. 'I'll speak to the other ladies. We're going shopping together today.' She gave me that cheeky grin. 'Oh John, we are going to have to leave you men together.' She put her hand to her forehead, looked down slightly, like an actor on a stage. 'How are you going to manage without us? We are going to be gone a whole four hours!' Mary giggled as she went into the cabin to get dressed.

Later that day while the women were shopping, the men went to the local pub. We sat looking out over the harbour discussing our trip home, and what islands we were going to stop at. We were all totally relaxed.

One of our companions turned to me, 'John, you're retired aren't you?'

'Yes, I am,' I replied.

'I am on long service leave and have been discussing with my wife Jane about retiring,' he told me. 'I've been with the one company all my working life and I can see many changes I don't like. For instance the lack of integrity. What we design and develop we think is ours. All the work we put into developing and testing to make sure our product is right, then somebody from overseas will manufacture the same thing. They cut back on the structural design and sell it cheap, and it's our reputation that suffers. We can't compete with them and we have no protection through our government systems. I look at you and Mary and think that maybe Jane and I should be doing the same thing.'

'Looking at your age and looking at Jane, I think you would be doing the right thing. Mary and I are so much happier spending this time together. I was frightened about what I was going to do after retiring, but I'm not now. I'm really enjoying it.'

A taxi pulled up and we saw the women getting out with all their packages. They were all laughing and giggling. I think the cab driver was glad to see the last of them. I watched Mary trying to reach into her handbag to pay for the cab, but the bundles and packages were hindering her. All four women laughed even louder. Mary looked up and nodded in our direction. We stood up and looked at each other. One of the men said, 'Well, that's our freedom gone!' All four of us chuckled.

As we were leaving, Nigel and one of the other men who was a seasoned sailor said, 'We know where there is a beautiful island. If you take a few 4 litre drums of fresh water, the inhabitants of the island would appreciate it.'

Two days later we anchored in a beautiful cove. The island was about 4 kilometres long and 1 kilometre at the widest part. It was covered in beautiful palm trees. Nigel had his small dinghy out and was putting some 4 litre drums of water into it. I counted six. Nigel, and his wife Maree rowed to the shore.

A man with a long white beard and a woman, obviously very fit, ran down the beach to meet them. They all embraced each other, laughing and giggling. Nigel pointed in our direction. The man with the white beard waved to us, and gestured, inviting us on to the shore. Before we knew it, we were all sitting around a fire, drinking wine and laughing. Lucy, the lady who lived on the island was Maree's sister. They hadn't seen each other for about five years. The most precious thing to the islanders was fresh water, so they appreciated our gift.

'What brings you to this island?' Mary asked Lucy.

'Well, a few years ago there was a recession. My husband and I owned a very successful company. We were doing core soil samples for buildings and many other projects in the agricultural industry, but the bank had control of us financially, they shut us down at the beginning of the recession. We found out what the bank had done to us was illegal and were paid compensation. We had wanted to get out of the rat race, so with the money we received we bought this island. Now we make a little bit of money to pay our way, but we are free. We don't have to answer to anybody, and my husband is all mine!' Lucy leaned over and nudged him in his side and gut. 'But he can't catch me!'

He looked at her through his big bushy eyebrows. 'But I can when I want too!'

Lucy leaned over and kissed him on the end of his nose. 'With a little help from me!'

We stayed another full day and the following morning set sail for the next island. It's very hard to leave paradise, but it was nice to meet some like-minded people. Our calculations told us we should arrive in the evening. We had full sail up so as not to waste any time. Mary was below deck doing all the chores that a man is useless at doing. According to her men never do it properly, and she would ask why men always grin when women mention it.

As I stood thinking, I noticed a white dot in the distance and wondered what it was. I picked up the old man's binoculars, and to my amusement, I found that if I placed my arms just in front of the wheel there were two indentations for my elbows, and the binoculars rested nicely just in front of my eyes. Without thinking I said out loud 'You did a nice job, that's very good.'

'Of course I did boy, comfort is the name of the game.'

That sent a shiver down my spine, but I didn't turn around.

The white dot got bigger as we got closer to it. At first I thought it was my imagination. A pelican? It wouldn't be a pelican again, would it? The white dot was standing on something, but I couldn't see what it was. The charts don't show any sandbanks, rocks of reefs around here. We were getting closer and I had to make a decision, but what? Then I noticed a long object making the water's movement change. Could it be a dead whale? I didn't know the answer to my question. I shouted out to Mary to hold onto something tight.

Mary's voice came back. 'Why John?'

I didn't have time to reply. I'd already started to turn the wheel to starboard, to keep the wind in the sails so I had good movement in the vessel. I could hear something sliding off the table onto the floor and heard Mary's voice shout out 'Damn, damn, f***.' That was a word I didn't believe I had ever heard Mary say. Michael the Coast Guard did say she's normal now.

I still couldn't make out what the long object was, but it was far too close for comfort. I turned a little more to starboard and hoped there was nothing hanging off the mystery object. It was about 40 foot or 12 metres, and ugly. That's all I could say, ugly. Mary appeared out of the cockpit, she had two lifejackets and was balancing herself to the lean of the vessel. She shouted to me, 'What's wrong John?'

I pointed 'That's what's wrong!' Mary went to the port side, hanging on to the cockpit rail with both hands.

'What is it?' I was just about to say I don't know, when Mary's voice rose high, 'the pelican John! The pelican.'

Just then the pelican flew off and headed towards land. I was busy concentrating on the object in the water.

'John was that my pelican?' Mary asked.

'I don't know Mary. I don't know.'

Then I noticed that the floating object was covered in barnacles and seaweed. It was a huge tree trunk with small roots sticking out from one end and one branch rising up in the air.

'Mary, could you please get me a scotch and dry. I need it!' Mary looked at me, puzzled, and went below to get me a scotch and dry. By the time she had come back up I had all sails in and had started the motor. I reached out and took the drink and knocked it back.

'Mary, if that pelican had not been on that tree trunk, we would have hit it.' Mary looked back at the tree trunk.

'Was that my pelican?'

'I don't know dear. I'm going to take the rope and that yellow ball and tie it to the tree trunk so other boats don't hit it.'

I made a noose in one end of the rope; the ball was on the other. I put the little motor into reverse and used the movement of the water to keep the boat off the tree trunk. I asked Mary to hold the ball while I threw the loop over the branch and pulled it tight. 'You can throw the ball in now Mary.' She dropped the ball in the water so quickly as though it was red hot! I put the motor into forward and moved well away from the tree trunk, and then slipped into neutral and left the motor in idle, just in case.

I went down below and called the coastguard to inform them what had happened. I told them I had tied a yellow ball to the tree trunk. They gave me a very nice 'thank you' and said they would take care of the problem. I turned the little motor off and set all our sails and we were on our way again. I couldn't get the pelican out of my mind. If the pelican hadn't been there, if the pelican hadn't... I said to myself, I love pelicans.

I heard Mary's voice speaking on the radio. The lady she was talking to said they were worried when they heard us calling the coast guard. They stayed on the radio chatting, Deanna, Anthony's wife asked me whether it was the same Pelican, I replied 'I think so, but I don't really know'

All the other women gave their opinions, they all agreed it was the same Pelican, this made me very, very happy. They stayed chatting until we arrived at the island later in the evening.

All the boats were anchored in a beautiful little cove. We were well protected from the weather. That night we all sat on the beach sipping good wine and discussing the events of the day.

Tony grinned and said to me, 'Would you swap this for the office, John?'

I thought of the events that had happened today. 'Tony, today I lived, I was alive, I wouldn't change it for the world.'

'I'll be back in the office next week John, I'll be thinking of you,' Tony said with a sad look in his eye.

I put my hand on his shoulder. 'Your turn will come. At least now you know what you'll do in your retirement. It's something to work towards.'

'Yes John,' Tony nodded.

There was a small cold front coming up the coast with some wind. We all discussed it and decided that we should stay here for the next three days. Mary's voice boomed out. With a chuckle she said, 'we sorted that out well, didn't we girls?' They all got up and ran into the water, laughing, giggling and splashing each other.

Tony laughed. 'They're a queer lot, those women, aren't they? They never sit still and take it easy.' He reached into his bag and took out another bottle of wine, laughed and said, 'This is hard work isn't it?'

The next morning when I went up on deck , *My Lady's* stern was facing the beach. So were the sterns of the other yachts. We all had a marvellous view of the island. This beautiful cove seemed to be designed just for yachts. We could swing around at anchor with the tide without interfering with the other yachts. Mary came up alongside me wearing a two-piece bathing suit. She nudged me in the shoulder, 'John, if we were here alone I would only need one piece!'

'Mary, I will tell the others to leave now!' I laughed.

Mary chuckled. 'You do that John, you do that!' She dived over the side and swam to the shore, then she stood up and placed both hands either side of her top and winked at me, put her head slightly to one side and grinned. I nodded. 'John, I'm going to get some coconuts and make something for breakfast.'

I shouted out 'Mary let me get the hard-hat; too many people have been hurt by falling coconuts.'

I went below and came back up with the hard-hat and threw it to Mary. She picked it up and looked at it, gave me a funny look and placed it over her breast. She shouted, 'Do you have another one John?' She giggled as she put it on her head and trotted over to the nearest coconut palm. As I stood watching her I thought to myself 'you wouldn't think she was the same woman; she seems so totally at peace with herself. I love her new-found sense of humour.'

Nigel's yacht was anchored to my left, or our port. It was more designed for racing with a big steering wheel at the stern. Nigel was sitting on top of the cockpit, sipping a cup of coffee. I saw a big log lying on the beach. Nigel saw it at the same time. It sent a shiver up my spine. I started to panic and tried to think of what could I do. The log had moved and one end of it lifted up into the air. I tried to shout to Mary, but no sound was coming out of my mouth. I shook myself out of my panic and shouted again, 'Mary, stay where you are, don't move!'

She stood up and looked at me. 'Why John?' I pointed down the beach and shouted again. 'Don't move Mary!'

Then she saw the big salt water crocodile. It had opened his mouth wide and lifted itself up on its front legs and was watching her. I ran to the bow of *My Lady* and let out another four or five metres of chain, locked it tight, and ran back to the stern. *My Lady* drifted onto the beach. My chest was tight and I felt weak in the legs. I looked over towards the crocodile and noticed Nigel had a 303 rifle jungle carbine in his hands. I recognised the rifle straight away because my dad had one. Nigel put the bullet clip in and pressed it into the home position. I could nearly hear it click. He lifted the bolt up on the barrel, slid it back, allowing a bullet to go into the bridge, then he pushed the bolt forwards, pushing the bullet home, then pushing the bolt back down. Nigel turned his head towards me and gave a small nod, then took aim at the crocodile. His wife was standing behind him with her hands up to her mouth.

'Mary, don't run, just walk slowly towards me,' I shouted. She started walking slowly toward me. The crocodile was watching her. I wanted to jump over the side and go to her, but that would provoke the crocodile, so I didn't. I had a lump in my throat as big as an orange. I remember saying to myself, 'Hold it John, don't panic'. Mary had reached the edge of the water. I put my arms out so she could reach them. I seized both her wrists and heaved her out of the water and onto the deck. We hugged each other and then Mary said 'John, what about my coconuts?'

'There was a damn fourty-four foot crocodile waiting to have you for breakfast and all you're worried about are your bloody coconuts!'

'John, it wasn't fourty-four foot long. There's no need to exaggerate!'

'Mary, in my mind, at the moment, it was even bigger than that!'

Suddenly the trauma of it hit her and she started to collapse at the knees. I reached out and held her, glancing back over towards Nigel. He was grinning at me, the rifle was down by his side. His wife was holding his hand. I reached out and put my thumb in the air and shook my head. Then I gestured to him with my hand to say shall we have a drink. He returned the gesture by putting his finger to his thumb and raising it into the air.

Everybody came aboard *My Lady* and we sat quietly talking about the yacht club. I was trying to find out more information, but no-one could help me. I noticed Anthony and his wife Deanna listening to me very carefully. They were a quiet couple, both in their seventies. I tried to read them psychically. Anthony was a very studious man, full of knowledge which he used in many different ways. He had high morals; he had seen the world and had known hard knocks. Their yacht was comfortable, not a racer, but well cared for, well stocked. His wife Deanna had been a secretary, always busy, everything always ready. Anthony just had to put his hand out and whatever he needed was there.

The days seemed to slide past. I was enjoying the conversations, but my mind had started to wander. He was there, he was there! 'Well boy, have you learned anything over the last two days? Sharpened you up a bit didn't it? A little bit different from the office.' I took a deep breath, but I knew he had gone. He was right. The events of the past few days had shaken me up. I had felt pressure during my working life, but not like this. This was totally different. One minute totally relaxed, not a care in the world. The next, right on a knife's edge, face-to-face with a problem. Different to being in a boardroom playing politics with other people's resources and money. Dealing with people who had no morals and no conscience; just greed and no responsibility. This was real life; having to make quick decisions. You can't play politics at sea. I glanced over at the crocodile; he was asleep. He must have crawled up on to the island for a rest. There weren't any turtles here for him to feed on. This island is rightfully his.

Next morning, instead of sleeping in we took our coffee, and bacon and eggs, up into the cockpit so that we could enjoy looking at the idyllic island, so that it would remain in our minds forever. The big crocodile had gone, but the question was, where?

Mary and I prepared the yacht for sea. We were planning on leaving early the next morning. We wanted everything to be shipshape. I'm starting to like this new language. Shipshape, it says a lot.

We were all sitting on the sand relaxing. I looked at Anthony, he was wearing his old pair of trackie dacks, a floppy T-shirt and an old straw hat on his head. There was something familiar about this man. He reminded me of Sir Winston Churchill, but then again, I could see Sir Robert Menzies in him too. What was that telling me? 'John, sharpen yourself up, you used to be good at this, is he a politician? I would bet my bottom dollar he is.' His wife was definitely a secretary.

Nigel's voice spoke up. 'There's a large vessel coming from the mainland, and it's coming straight here.' We watched it get bigger as it got closer. 'It's the Coast Guard, maybe letting us know that we can only anchor here for so many days at a time,' Nigel said.

The captain of the Coast Guard vessel would have known these waters as he came right up on to the beach, touching his bow up against a sandbank. A man climbed down off the bow with a briefcase; it didn't look normal. He walked up to us. 'Good Afternoon Ladies, Gentlemen, enjoy your stay.' He was too polite, a smoothie. He looked at Anthony.

Deanna's voice boomed out, 'Can't you leave him alone for a minute? All he wanted was a few days break, but you can't even let him have that.'

'It's all right, it's all right,' Anthony said quietly. He looked at the man. 'What do you want?'

I looked at both of them. Who is this man? Are they enemies, or are they friends?

Deanna's voice boomed out again. 'You give a man The Order of Australia and a few other fancy titles and you believe you own him. He needs his rest and relaxation. I'm furious that you can't leave him alone.'

Anthony took her hand. 'Not now dear, this man is just doing his job.' He winked at the man. I'm sure he didn't enjoy the boat ride out to this beautiful island. 'Henry, what do you want?' Henry opened his briefcase and took out a thick envelope and handed it to Anthony who read through the papers very carefully. He put his hand up and Henry gave him a black Texta. Anthony crossed out words or lines, then he gave the Texta back, his hand still outstretched. Henry put a pin into it. Anthony glanced at me, 'Could you come and co-sign this please to say it is me signing it?' I didn't argue with him. I signed it where he told me to sign; he then signed it and gave it back to Henry, who put it back into his briefcase and buckled it up. 'Thank you Sir Anthony.'

Anthony chuckled, 'A feather in your hat Henry. She didn't think you'd get me to sign it.' He gave one of those Sir Winston Churchill chuckles. Henry bowed slightly and returned to the vessel, and they were gone.

Anthony looked over towards me 'You talked about the Yacht Club, John that document was in your favour. The man who originally owned *My Lady* was my friend.' He sat down, pulled his hat down over his eyes a bit more, and held up his hand. Deanna gave him a drink. He laughed and said, 'You shifty old bugger, that was a nice bit of work!' Nobody else knew who he was talking to, they thought he was talking to himself but I knew he was talking to the old man, and so did Mary.

Next day we were enjoying the trip back home to Sydney. Mary spent time talking to the women on the radio, just small talk about their world, which was mainly looking after us men.

Before we knew it we reached the entrance to Sydney Harbour. The Coathanger (Sydney Harbour Bridge) was coming into view. Although Mary and I were tired we were so happy and proud of our Sydney Harbour.

Malcolm was there waiting to meet us, ready to tie up our bow line.

'Good evening John, Mary.'

'Good evening Malcolm.'

'I think you're back just in time, there's a big storm coming over.'

'Yes Malcolm, I've been watching it. Come aboard and have a drink.'

'Thanks John.'

I was waiting for the old man to say something, but Malcolm had already slipped his shoes off. 'The old man is not going to tell me off John,' he grinned and winked at me. I shook my head. Malcolm sat down on one of the soft cushions.

'How was your trip John?' Mary's voice broke in before I could answer and for the next hour I just nodded my head backwards and forwards, or up and down. Her voice was full of passion and enthusiasm. The way she moved her arms up and down gesturing, I thought, next time the University wants a lecturer, I might put her forward. She's certainly doing a good job now. Abruptly Mary stopped her story, looked at Malcolm and said 'I will go and get some supper for us all,' and with that she disappeared into the galley.

I grinned at Malcolm. He gave a small chuckle and said, 'I think Mary enjoyed herself John.

'Yes, she did. She made some good friends on the other yachts. I know those women are planning something for us men. Where we will end up, God only knows.'

'John, when you were away those three men I told you about before, came back. They asked me when you would be back. I said I didn't know and the one who seemed to be in charge said to me in a very arrogant manner, I want the exact date they will be back, I've got business to do and it can't wait! So when will they be back? I said to the arrogant sod, how long is a piece of string, tell me that and perhaps I might have an answer for you. I turned and walked away from him. I'm supposed to keep my cool and be polite, but that one pushed the boundaries. One of them gave me a business card and told me to phone them as soon as you got back, but I seemed to have lost the card!'

I reached over and put my hand on Malcolm's shoulders. 'Would you like another drink?'

'Yes please John.' We both grinned at each other. Mary came up with our supper and we had a very good evening.

The next day Mary and I discussed what we had to do. Mary wanted to see the grandchildren and our daughter and son. I told Mary that I wanted to put *My Lady* up on a slip. Up north there's woodworm in the creeks and streams, and because she's make of wood I wanted her hull cleaned and freshly painted with antifouling. I also wanted her rigging checked over.

'Does that mean we could take off at a moment's notice?' Mary said giving me that sideways glance.

'Yes, Mary, it does.'

'Then we can stay with the children John, I'll arrange it. Two nights?'

'I don't know Mary, I'll check.'

I rang the shipyard where *My Lady* was built; Malcolm had given me the phone number. 'Yes Sir, our slipway is empty at the moment, two days should be sufficient. It will be nice to have her back. We built her and she is the very best.'

The next day Mary had taken off in the car to spend the day with the children. I shouted out to Malcolm 'I'm taking *My Lady* over to the slipway, would you like to come?' Malcolm let the bow lines go and was aboard before I could blink! The little motor once again gently took us out of the pod and into the harbour. We sailed under Sydney Harbour Bridge, I looked up and felt a sense of pride. Its construction was a marvel.

Soon *My Lady* was in the dry dock, sitting high and dry out of the water. Men were already cleaning her hull. A man came onboard and introduced himself. 'Hi my name is Fred.'

'I'm John,' I said as we shook hands.

'John, I'm the shipwright and I helped build this yacht, or should I say Schooner. Is there anything you need done?'

'Yes thanks Fred. Could you please check her rigging for me and have somebody go over her electrics?'

'Sure John. We can have that done.'

'Fred, if you say you had a part in building *My Lady*, you may be able to answer some questions for me. See where the bench goes up to the bulkhead, the cupboard underneath it stops short of the bulkhead, but there is a panel there.'

'John, slide your hand up to the top of the cupboard nearest the bulkhead. Now put your hand up into the corner and you will feel a small brass lever. Slide it towards the bulkhead.' The panel between the cupboard and the bulkhead sprung open. I stared at it for a few moments, and then looked inside. There were files of paperwork and a good bottle of brandy.

Fred grinned at me. 'That shifty old sod had many tricks up his sleeve. Above the forward cabin door there is a large beam beautifully carved in panels. Come with me John.' I followed him to the forward cabin. 'Put your hand up there, do you feel the brass knob?'

'Yes, I do.'

'Push it to the starboard.' Just then the panels flew open. There were more documents and papers inside. 'Just push on them to close the panels. Now come down to the galley.'

When we got into the galley Fred said, 'See where the cups hang on their hooks, lift them off. Inside there were more documents. Same thing John, there is a little brass lever on the top panel, just push it closed and it will lock in by itself.'

I put the cups back on their hooks and shook my head. Fred started to leave, when he got to the top of the stairs he turned around, looked at me and winked. 'Be careful John, the old man would have thought well into the future. He was always playing games with people.' Then he disappeared.

Two days later *My Lady* was back in her pod. Mary and I were having coffee in the cockpit when a familiar voice startled me. 'John, could we have a word with you please?'

I looked out at the jetty. There was that slippery, arrogant and sly man with his wig perched nicely on top of his head. He was with two other well-dressed gentlemen.

'I was hoping I wouldn't meet you again. What do you want?'

'Can I come on board and talk with you?'

I said it before I realised what I was saying. 'Take those blasted shoes off; you don't come aboard a vessel with shoes on like that!'

He looked at me, startled. Mary started to giggle, but put her hand to her mouth. He took his shoes off and stepped on board.

'John, I will not waste your time. I had business with the gentleman who previously owned this vessel. When you bought this vessel did you find any paperwork?'

I thought of the secret compartments. 'No, when we came on board this vessel we only found some shipping charts and papers relating to the vessel sales. That's all. Oh yes, and the logbook for the motor.'

'Well John, if you should find any documents, they belong to me.' He was angry and annoyed when they left. I watched them stop at the gate to the jetty and talk to Malcolm. I wanted to get up and go and look at the papers and documents, then thought better of it. That's what they would expect me to do and they would be watching.

Mary was looking at me. 'What are you up to John?'

'Mary if we could have another cup of coffee, I'll tell you.' We had our coffee and Mary was totally intrigued.

'John, when can we look?'

'They are still at the gate watching us. I think we should wash the windows on the cabin, don't you?' Mary gave me that annoying look.

'Well, I was going to wash them anyway, but if you do them, remember I will have to do them again. Men can't clean windows!' We spent the next two hours washing windows.

When we were finished I said to Mary, 'I want to talk to Malcolm first before we look at the documents.'

'Malcolm, those three men that came down to the jetty, have you seen them before?'

'Yes, John, they were the three looking at your car. They wanted to know where you were and when you would be back.'

'Did they ask you anything just now?'

'Yes John, they are a nosey lot. I told them to mind their own business. What you do has got nothing to do with me.

One of them said it could be profitable to me and that's when I told them where to go.'

'Thanks Malcolm.'

'Any time John'.

I went back to *My Lady* and with Mary I opened the first compartment under the bench. The little door sprung open. Mary nearly knocked me over trying to see inside. She lifted out the first file and put it on the bench. I leant against her to look at the file. She gave a small giggle. 'No. John, I got it out first!' She was excited.

'Whatever you say Madam, whatever you say!' I smiled and stepped back.

Mary started to read the first document. A serious expression came over her face. 'John, these are all legal papers, I don't understand them.'

'Give me the next document Mary.' She handed it to me and I studied it for a moment.

'What does it mean John? It is obviously a title, but to what?'

'Mary, it's the title to the yacht club! The owners are the members of the yacht club. The old man was holding it in trust.'

Mary slid the next file over to me and I glanced through it. 'Mary, put the file back into the cabinet. I want to go up and talk to the people in the yacht club and ask a few tactful questions.'

She studied me for a few moments. 'Okay John, but I want to come up with you,' she said as she put the file back into the cabinet.

'Just click it closed with your finger,' I told her.

We went up into the cockpit. Mary asked me, 'Do you think we should lock *My Lady* up?'

'No,' I answered, 'that would be too obvious. They would think we'd found something.'

We walked up to the yacht club and went into the lounge bar. I noticed the condition of the paintwork and gutters around the roof and window frames. The yacht club needed a lot of maintenance done. Mary and I walked up to the bar and ordered a drink. I put my hand out to shake the barman's hand. 'I believe you're Frank?' I said.

'And you're John?' he replied.

'Yes, I am.'

Frank asked me, 'How are you enjoying *My Lady*, John? He glanced at Mary.

'We are totally in love with her,' Mary replied smiling.

Frank grinned at us both. 'I think the old man chose you two.'

'Frank, could we ask you a couple of small questions?'

'Fire away John.'

'Who owns the yacht club?'

Frank's face went very serious and his eyes looked into mine. I knew he was asking himself whether he should talk, whether he could trust us and what were our motives. 'Frank you can trust us,' I said.

Frank took a deep breath. 'We don't know who owns the yacht club, but we know the local people raised the money and built it. But who owns the harbour trust lease, we don't know. In the past there was a lot of talk about pulling the club down and building private apartments here with their own moorings. The old man was against it. There was supposed to be a committee meeting, but at the last moment it was cancelled. That was just after the old man died. There was a whisper going around that three men were looking for some documents.'

Frank had a deep look of sadness on his face. He looked up at me. 'We raised the money to build this yacht club, it doesn't belong to any one person. It belongs to the members, for the members. This is their yacht club. Nobody has the right to play games with it.' I reached across the bar and put my hand on his shoulder.

'Mary and I are also members. Come on Mary, we've got work to do. See you shortly Frank. I'll keep you informed.'

Mary was already walking towards the door. She hadn't finished her gin and tonic. 'Mary, do you want to finish your drink?'

'No John, we've got too much work to do.'

I thought to myself, what have I done? I could tell my people what to do, when and how, but to tell Mary? What have I done!

Mary was down the steps into the galley before me. 'John, John, how do I open it?'

I smiled. 'I thought we might have lunch at Doyle's before we go through the paperwork.'

Mary put her hands on her hips. 'John, do you want a kick in the ankle?' I couldn't help myself, I burst out laughing. This is my Mary, the Mary I married, full of spice and life.

'Put your hand up inside the cupboard to the corner, there is a small brass knob, push it. The little cupboard door sprung open, and Mary had both files out. We went through the second file. It contained the papers and documents for the Harbour Trust. The yacht club had a 99 year lease, and as far as I could make out, any building that stood there and called itself the yacht club would be legal and would be entitled to the lease.

'This is getting too complicated Mary. I understand this, but I don't understand it. It's how it is interpreted legally. There are too many twists and turns. Let's look in the other cupboards.'

We went into the forward cabin, pushed the little brass knob and the little panel sprung open. Mary lifted out the role of papers and she spread them on the bed. 'Mary, these are plans for a new yacht club, the permit from the Council, and from the Ports and Harbours. I think we'd better get the papers to somebody who knows what they're doing. There's only one person we can totally trust with this.'

Mary started laughing. 'That's Terry, isn't it?'

I picked up my phone and called him. He answered straight away. 'Terry, its John here.'

'John, how can I help you?'

I replied 'How about lunch today at Doyle's, say 1 pm? I know you like seafood.'

'What are you up to John?'

'Just playing the same game Terry.'

'Thanks for getting me out of the boardroom meeting. I'll meet you there.'

'I will get your briefcase John,' Mary said.

'No, don't. As far as anybody is concerned we are having lunch at Doyle's with a friend. Why don't we just put the documents in your bag, the one that Mary Poppins gave you. If anybody saw us with a briefcase they might put two and two together, and Mary, we haven't looked in the other compartments yet.

'I'll make coffee,' Mary said as she put the kettle on.

Mary could see the concern on my face. 'What's wrong John?'

'I don't know. I just get the feeling we are being watched.' Then I saw Malcolm coming down the jetty towards us. 'Mary could you go up into the cockpit and ask Malcolm whether he would like a cup of coffee.' Her head went back slightly and she looked at me with a puzzled expression. She went up into the cockpit and called Malcolm over. I saw him nod to her and I took down three mugs. Malcolm came down into the cabin.

'Good day John. If you look over into the next property there is a man with a pair of binoculars, he's been there most of the day, but he's always looking in this direction.'

I glanced over Malcolm's shoulder and there he was. The kettle started to boil and as I made the coffee I tried to think. Mary was watching me with a serious look. I slid my mobile phone across the bench to her.

'You don't like perverts do you dear, why don't you complain.' Mary grinned at me and winked to Malcolm.

She dialled a number. 'Is this the Police?'

'My name is Mary. We live aboard a yacht or rather, it's a schooner, and its name is *My Lady*. There is a man watching me with a pair of binoculars in the next property. I can't sunbathe with him watching me all the time. Is there anything you can do for me? I'm so frightened, and want to know why he's watching me.'

'Madam, give me the full address. We will have somebody over there to take care of it for you.'

Mary gave him the address and a description of the man, and her mobile phone number. With a sweet innocent voice she said, 'Thank you so much. I feel so much safer now.'

'Any time Madam. It's a pleasure to help you.'

We discreetly watched the man as we drank our coffee and were surprised how quickly a police boat turned up. A policeman was walking down the jetty to where the man was. He had nowhere to go, the police talked to him for a few minutes then they boarded the police boat and were gone.

Malcolm chuckled, 'I don't think I'll get on the wrong side of you Mary.' He turned and started to walk back to his office.

'Malcolm, thank you.'

'Thank you, John and Mary. I enjoyed that.' With that he went back up the jetty to his office. I took down the other cups and pushed the little brass button, the panel sprung open. Mary beat me to it. She was on tiptoes, took the documents out and put them on the table.

'What are they John, what are they?'

'Mary, do stop bouncing up and down and give me a moment.' I went through the papers. I went through them again and again. 'Mary, these papers are the finances to build the new clubhouse. I think he had everything tied up in a nice little bundle, all neat and tidy. Shifty old fox.'

My mind raced back to when I first stepped out onto the veranda and saw the name *My Lady* for sale. A shiver went up my spine. I looked down at the documents. How did he get into my mind, how did he get there? Mary's voice broke in.

'We'd better go dear if we're going to get to Doyle's on time. You know how punctual Terry is.'

We were already seated when Terry arrived. I shook his hand and Mary and Terry embraced each other.

Terry sat down. 'Come on John, tell me what you're up to.'

'You have a very suspicious mind Terry.'

'How long have I known you John?' Terry said as Mary pulled the papers out of her bag.

Terry had a quick glance through them. He looked up at me, then at Mary. He reached inside his inside pocket, took out his mobile phone and dialled a number.

'Good afternoon Peter. You know the problem we are having with the paperwork, a good friend of mine has it. He is completely trustworthy. We are at Doyle's now. Could you come over? Yes, yes, I will pay for the meal.'

Terry slipped his mobile phone back into his side pocket. 'John, you know Peter Smith, he is the best lawyer and barrister I've ever met, straight down the line.'

'Yes Terry, I've used him quite a bit myself.'

'Well John, that slippery, slimy, little sod we both know had been trying to manipulate the yacht club to suit his own ends. Another lawyer had the paperwork and he died. Nobody knew where it was. Where did you find it?'

'On the Schooner. *My Lady* had it all the time.'

'How long have you been on board the vessel? How long have you owned it? No, never mind. Let Peter sort this out.'

Peter quickly arrived and glanced around the restaurant. 'Nothing like a free lunch Terry. Oh Mary, John, how are you both. I heard you did a bit of sailing.'

Terry's voice broke in 'They bought *My Lady*.'

Peter stood straight and looked at me very seriously, and grinned at Mary. Then he turned to Terry, 'You say you have the paperwork?'

'Yes, Peter. John and Mary have the paperwork.'

A small grin came over Peter's face. 'Terry, a double scotch please.'

Terry replied, 'I said a free lunch, not free drinks. You are very expensive when it gets to drinks.'

Peter sat down in the chair waving the back of his hand towards Terry. 'Stop quibbling man, I need a drink. John, Mary, there were a number of us who raised the money to build that yacht club, for the average man, they built it, and it belongs to them. The old man was one of them. We have been fighting to maintain it. He had raised the money but just before we were going to have a meeting, he died. We thought all was lost. There is a 99 year lease from the Harbour Trust that is the key. Do you have it?'

'Yes, we do,' I smiled.

'What are you going to do with it?' Peter asked.

Mary's voice broke in, 'Give it to its rightful owners and build a new yacht club to the specifications and plans that we have.'

Terry was coming back with the drinks on a tray. Peter didn't look up, he just reached out, took his drink, and swallowed half of it. He looked seriously at both of us, with that barrister look. 'John, Mary, I never liked that shifty old sod, always ten steps ahead of me. I know why he picked you two. John how long have you legally owned this vessel?'

I took my papers out of my inside pocket and handed them to him. He studied them. 'Then we are safe John.' He picked up his whisky glass again and swallowed the remains. He looked at us again very seriously. 'The money, where has he hidden the money?'

'Peter, we have it.'

Peter's eyes widened. Terry was shaking his head. A big grin spread over Peter's face. 'Terry, another drink.'

Peter's eyes widened. Terry was shaking his head. A big grin spread over Peter's face. 'Terry, would you like another drink?'

Terry stared at him. 'Look on the table. I know you will only have ten drinks tonight, so I got you another,' he laughed. 'Here,' he said as he pushed a glass towards Peter.

'I think I could speak on behalf of everybody here,' Peter glanced at Terry, 'John, would you accept the responsibility of building the new yacht club?'

Mary's voice broke in. 'Yes, he will. It will be for the men and women, or should I say, it will be for the women and men of the yacht club.'

I sat there shaking my head. 'This is going to be a nightmare because I'm not really in charge, am I?'

Peter and Terry were looking at me with grins on their faces.

'John, if you would intrust the paperwork to us, we would very much appreciate it. But you keep the plans, you'll need them,' Peter said.

Terry looked down at the Mary Poppins bag. 'Peter you will look so good carrying a Mary Poppins bag. Very professional.'

Peter looked at him, annoyed. 'Terry, order the meal. I'll have the crab and another scotch, that should take the grin off your face. A big crab Terry!'

Peter looked at me puzzled. He was studying me, and he pushed a blank piece of paper and a pen over to me. 'Could you please show me your signature on this piece of paper.'

Peter studied the signature for a moment, then he reached into his inside pocket and took out a document. He read the signature at the bottom of the page. 'John, have you ever met Vivian?'

I frowned at him. 'I don't know the name.'

Peter shook his head with a bit of annoyance 'Yes, I understand John. Vivian never uses his first name, it's the name his mother gave him and he hates it. You know the old Johnny Cash song, a boy named Sue, how do you do. Vivien only uses his last name, Anthony.'

'Yes Peter, that makes sense now. We did wonder why one moment he was Anthony and the next he was Sir Anthony.'

'That's our man John. You signed a document with him?'

'Yes Peter.' I lowered my head thinking this is getting like a Court Room and it's annoying. 'A large coast guard boat came up to the island and a man by the name of Henry stepped off of it with a briefcase.' Peter started to chuckle. 'Sir Anthony read through some paperwork, made a few alterations, gave it back to him and he disappeared back to the mainland.'

Peter grinned. 'And Vivian was on his yacht?'

'Yes Peter.'

'That is a feather in Henry's hat,' Mary whispered in my ear.

Peter looked at me quite seriously. 'There is this woman, for legal reasons I cannot mention her name, but she thought Sir Anthony was out of the way, on holidays. Nobody knew where he had gone. So she thought she was playing her trump card trying to change the structure of the Harbour Trust. But John, with this document Sir Anthony and you signed, and who would argue with your signature. There is nothing to block the yacht club re-build anymore. John, I saw that old man at the morgue, I was at his funeral. He is dead, but I don't believe it. That shifty old sod is still here, and still ten steps in front of me.'

Mary and I looked at each other, raised our eyebrows, but said nothing. Then Mary made a statement. 'There will be a veranda on the back of the Yacht Club.'

Mary and I eventually returned to *My Lady*. We went through the gate to the jetty. Malcolm wasn't in his office and we could hear a big commotion on the jetty. Then we saw Malcolm, he was fighting off a pelican.

Mary shouted, 'No, no Malcolm.' She ran down the jetty and pushed Malcolm to one side. She knelt down in front of the pelican and it hopped up onto her knees and rested its head on her shoulder. She gently picked up the pelican in her arms and very tenderly spoke to it. 'Oh, my little darling, I've missed you. I've been wondering how you were, but you are looking very well. I will have a serious talk with Malcolm to make sure he doesn't attack my pelican with a broom again.'

Malcolm yelled, 'He attacked me, I never attacked him!'

Mary turned around and looked at Malcolm with a smile. She winked at him. 'But you had the broom Malcolm!' Mary stood up and walked back down the little jetty to *My Lady* cuddling the pelican. 'I have a nice tin of pilchards just for you, and a small something to drink.' The pelican's reaction seemed to tell us he knew exactly what she was saying. It lifted its beak into the air and seemed to make a clapping sound. I started to follow Mary, not looking at Malcolm.

'Coffee Malcolm?' I wasn't acknowledging that anything unusual had happened. Malcolm was totally confused.

'Yes John, but not coffee, something stronger.

The months slid by quickly. I found so many old friends and colleagues who were willing to help us. We never received a bill for the machinery or for the crane. Some materials just seemed to appear. One or two councillors tried to play politics, as did some politicians, who thought they might get votes when they found out who was behind the yacht club. They backed off after one or two hiccups with the foundations. We did not scrimp with money and made the yacht club bigger, stronger and better.

One morning when Mary and I were having breakfast in the cockpit I said, 'Mary, the yacht club is finished, we have done our part, we have done our job, and this month is the right month for us to go now. How about the Cook Islands? How about we just leave?'

Mary walked over and kissed me on the end of my nose, and patted me on the top of my head.

'John, you can have command back. I've got some things to do to get ready, and I believe you have got some paperwork to finish. How about if we say three days?'

What could I say? 'Yes dear.'

Once again *My Lady* was at the mouth of Sydney Harbour heading out to sea. The sun was just rising over the horizon; we were listening to her sails once again. The old man sat in the cockpit with his arms around his wife. 'We are back at sea again dear, we are free, and we are alive!'

This is the end, or is it?

The End

www.ingramcontent.com/pod-product-compliance
Lightning Source LLC
Chambersburg PA
CBHW070630120726
47909CB00004B/1375